DATE DUE

GLENN GOULD
= AT WORK =
CREATIVE LYING

ANDREW KAZDIN

GLENN GOULD
= AT WORK =
CREATIVE LYING

E. P. DUTTON ⏀ NEW YORK

Published in the United States by E. P. Dutton,
a division of Penguin Books USA Inc.,
2 Park Avenue, New York, N.Y. 10016.

Published simultaneously in Canada by
Fitzhenry and Whiteside, Limited, Toronto.

Library of Congress Cataloging-in-Publication Data

Kazdin, Andrew.
    Glenn Gould at work : creative lying / Andrew Kazdin.
        p.   cm.
    Discography: p.
    ISBN 0-525-24817-X
    1. Gould, Glenn.   2. Pianists—Canada—Biography.   I. Title.
ML417.G68K4   1989
786.2'092—dc20
[B]   89-32524
                                                               CIP
                                                                MN

Designed by Earl Tidwell

1 3 5 7 9 10 8 6 4 2

First Edition

The excerpts from record liner notes on pages 3, 85–86, and 138–39
are quoted by permission of CBS Masterworks.

GLENN GOULD
= AT WORK =
CREATIVE LYING

1

I don't remember exactly when I met Glenn Gould, but it must have been sometime in late 1964. When I joined the staff of the Masterworks Department at Columbia Records in April of that year, Glenn was working with Paul Myers as his producer. I seem to recall that the second volume of the first book of *The Well-tempered Clavier* was just being released and the project that currently dominated their attention was the recording of the Bach Two- and Three-Part Inventions. The focus of attention at the time was the excessive amount of a sound coming from the piano, which Glenn finally nicknamed "hiccups." It is difficult to describe to one who has not had the firsthand pleasure exactly what a piano hiccup is, but since this mechanical phenomenon was to become our constant companion for several years, some sort of attempt is called for.

After the pianist's finger strikes a key, a remarkably complex Rube Goldberg–kind of chain reaction is set off inside the instrument that eventually culminates in a blow to the desired string by a felt-covered projectile called a "hammer." It is entirely appropriate to call this tone-instigator a "projectile" because, at the last moment, it really is a freewheeling missile completely out of the performer's control. You see, pianists can determine when to set off this event and can gauge the force with which they want the hammer to hit the string, but after it is launched, it reaches its target under its own steam.

The instant after it sets the string in vibration, the hammer must quickly come to a rest position, which allows it to be launched again if the pianist wishes to reiterate the note. Now, due to the particular hair-trigger condition that Gould wanted to feel beneath his touch as he played, the piano technician had to regulate the internal mechanism of the instrument into such a state that, on certain occasions, the hammer accidentally rebounded from its resting place and struck the string again in a kind of echo or shadow effect. Indeed, this often produced two notes for the price of one and, in rapid passages, could quite completely falsify the rhythmic scheme that the composer had in mind. This second, gratuitous attack became known as the "hiccup." Although Gould was probably the first to admit that he was not personally responsible for the *Doppelgänger*—the hammer having long since left his jurisdiction—and that its musical implications were in no way premeditated, the fact that the piano was indeed hiccuping was a sign that the mechanism had been regulated exactly to his specifications. Therefore these extra notes were to be looked upon as "friends."

Well, friends or no friends, I remember long editing sessions during which Glenn and Paul labored over the decision about whether or not to instruct the editing engineer to excise these interlopers using great care. This rather delicate operation carries with it the same risk as when a surgeon is trying to remove a brain tumor without accidentally taking away any brain in the same gesture. In any case, my earliest recollections of Glenn were centered on the Inventions recording where, it seems, the ubiquitous hiccups had reached a level of prominence and frequency intrusive enough to cause them to cross over into the "foe" category. Although many were removed, enough of the little buggers were left intact so that Gould wrote a "disclaimer" to be added to the liner notes. It stated, in part:

> Consequently, our enthusiasm for the rather extraordinary sound [the piano] now possessed allowed us to minimize the one minor after-effect which it had sustained—a slight nervous tic in the middle register which in slower passages can be heard emitting a sort of hiccup—and to carry on with the sessions without stopping to remedy this minor defect. I must confess that having grown somewhat accustomed to it I now find this charming idiosyncrasy entirely worthy of the remarkable instrument which produced it. . . . We would hope to preserve the present sound while reducing the hiccup effect so . . . "STAY TUNED IN— WE'RE FIXING IT."

In fact, future recordings contained few such hiccups, but when they appeared occasionally, Glenn always greeted them as one would long-lost friends.

Although I did not find out about it until much later (let's face it, the new junior Music Editor was not privy to the choicest bits of gossip), a certain amount of friction was developing between Glenn and Paul. Glenn never spoke about the cause for the eventual dissolution of their Artist/Producer relationship, but Paul once confided that he thought he knew the key event that had created a rift in the smooth-running atmosphere that was essential to Glenn's working method.

As I remember the way Paul had related it, the two had met in the recording studio to proceed with their projects. Soon after the start of the session, Glenn announced that he really didn't feel up to recording that day. This, in itself, was no earthshaking event because he had long since evinced a propensity for last-minute cancellations; but Gould went on to state that as long as the studio was available (and, to the continuing chagrin of the Masterworks Department, paid for) and the session had been aborted, perhaps he would continue to stay at the piano and practice. Paul agreed, but his mind was already focusing on a quantity of desk work that he needed to complete. He reasoned that the newfound free time would allow him to return to his office, twenty blocks uptown, and provide him with the opportunity to catch up on paperwork. Paul had started to say his farewells and take his leave when he became aware that Gould wanted his producer to stay and "watch him practice." Paul saw this as an unreasonable imposition on his time. It was bad enough that Glenn had rung up another studio cancellation bill, but now he was suggesting that Paul was to be deprived of the new plan to salvage his personal time. In a courteous but firm manner, Paul informed Glenn that he would decline the "invitation" and was going to catch a taxi uptown. Although he felt immediately that Gould was not pleased by the decision, the need for imposing a firm executive posture convinced Paul that he should not back down. In relating this story, Paul stated that this may have been "the beginning of the end" for their working relationship.

It must be understood that the only thing that changed between the two men was Glenn's desire to make further recordings with Paul as producer. In fact, the two of them continued a warm personal and business (discussing repertoire, planning future projects) relationship right to the end. Although this may seem like some sort of anomaly, it must be realized that the fundamental quality that Glenn's producer had to possess was the ability to bathe the recording studio in a kind of nonthreatening *Gemütlichkeit* in which Glenn could create his piano interpretations. If the "vibrations" were wrong, the sessions were doomed—and so was the producer.

Paul Myers was by no means Gould's first, or even primary, record producer. In 1955, when Glenn made his first recording for Columbia Masterworks *(Goldberg Variations)*, he was assigned Howard Scott as his "A & R (Artists and Repertoire) Man," and the two of them worked together for several years turning out approximately eleven records. I do not know the circumstances leading to their separation—unless it was Scott's departure from Columbia Masterworks—but Glenn then began work with a new man named Joseph Scianni. They collaborated on three and a half discs and apparently had entered into their next project *(The Well-tempered Clavier,* Book 1) when Paul Myers came onto the scene. The first volume of the Bach series bears both Scianni's and Myers's names as coproducers. Glenn spoke very little about the Scianni period, but he did tell me that dependability and neatness were not among Scianni's strong suits, and it is quite possible that these attributes formed the chief motivating factor in Gould's desire to start work with Paul.

Some time after the "watch-me-practice" event, Glenn began collaborating with Tom Frost as his producer. There were always at least two projects going at the same time, and Gould and Frost had launched into the Schönberg survey (all the solo piano works and all the songs with piano) and concurrently begun the set of Beethoven sonatas, opus 10. As I was then becoming active in the Masterworks Department and found that my primary assignment was to assist Tom Frost, it soon fell to my lot to do the editing work on the Beethoven set. The hiccup problem was not yet completely resolved and these three sonatas still exhibited a generous helping. Moreover, the creaking sounds being emitted by Glenn's favorite piano chair had reached an objectionably high level. Tom Frost, taking his cue from Gould's note explaining the hiccups, wrote his own little piece, which apologized to the listener for the snap, crackles, and pops. It had been decided to remove as many of these noises as possible, leaving only those that resisted the operation. Therefore, I found myself doing the "brain surgery" I had earlier observed Paul performing.

It was during this period of snipping extra notes and creaks out of the opus 10 sonatas that my friendship with Glenn began to develop. We were thrown together for extended periods of time working on Frost's record, and we seemed to get along amicably. Because of this, it was most natural for Frost to think of me when, on short notice before a scheduled session to record some more Schönberg *Lieder* (specifically the *Book of the Hanging Gardens,* opus 15), Frost could not direct the sessions and had to provide a substitute producer. It was the first time Glenn and I recorded together. With only one exception, this launched an exclusive collaboration that lasted through 1979 and produced over forty records.

These *Lieder* sessions took place on June 10 and 11, 1965, and progressed well. The music was not exactly easy, and it took hard work on my part to learn the score. The reader must understand that the record producer has to monitor all aspects of the recording session. Besides deciding the questions of sound quality and musical balance, it is important that a kind of running log be maintained relative to the musical performance itself. If any mistakes occur during a "take," notes are made so that in a subsequent taping, these slips can be corrected. Although the performer might be the first to become cognizant of these flaws, it is a bit much to expect total recall while a new take is in progress. Therefore, it is the producer's responsibility to remind the artist where special attention must be given. In order to do this, the producer has to have a rather thorough knowledge of the musical score. This task varies in difficulty in direct proportion to the complexity of the writing, and Schönberg always presents a challenge.

I was working with Helen Vanni—Glenn's soprano partner in the set—for the first time and found her to be a charming, hardworking, talented musician who proba-

6

bly singlehandedly did more to prepare me incorrectly for the true headaches of working with vocalists than any other performer. It was a great pleasure recording with her, and later we would repeat this collaboration several times as we worked to finish the complete set of *Lieder*.

As I recall, it wasn't until the second day that I discovered that Gould was not only playing the difficult piano part from memory but was equally expert in Helen's vocal line. In retrospect, this does not seem like an unusual event—commonplace only because Glenn always recorded without the printed score—but as it was my first encounter with *his* phenomenal memory, the event burned its way into *my* memory.

At the same time, I had my first exposure to another of Gould's unique obsessions: medical treatment. I still have a short bit of recorded tape that "eavesdropped" on a casual conversation between Gould and Vanni concerning therapy for bursitis that involved dipping the hands into molten paraffin. To this day, when I am forced to imagine this process, I cringe with all sorts of sympathetic pains that cause me to weigh the affliction against the cure! Glenn, however, discussed the procedure with dispassionate candor, and Helen listened and commented with the sort of emotional intensity that would accompany a lesson in furniture refinishing. Apparently she had "been there before" and learned to accept these medical diversions as part of working with Glenn Gould.

Sometime within the period that Glenn switched from Paul Myers to Tom Frost, one of the Schönberg works for solo piano was recorded with John McClure as producer. I was unaware of its existence until it just sort of bubbled to the surface as the editing was being done. You see, the way in which one collaborated with Tom Frost on an album was that he would record his part, then you would record your part, and them you would do the editing and mixing on both parts. You were then known as coproducers of the resultant product.

Thus it was with the Schönberg project. In actuality,

in order to release a set of records that would encompass the complete *Lieder* for voice and piano and the complete works for solo piano, three discs would be necessary. By choosing two of the three vocal works recorded by Frost and adding to that the long opus 15, which was the result of our first collaboration, one record of vocal music was ready. Also, if one collected the solo piano music already recorded by McClure and Frost and added the missing works, a second installment could be completed. So, rather than wait for the third record (of the remaining *Lieder*), the first two discs were planned as a two-record set.*

This also fit into the format of the continuing Schönberg series that was under way to record all the composer's output in an imposing collection of two-record boxes. Gould's contribution to that project would be known as volume 4. So, soon after the Gould-Vanni sessions, we scheduled the recording of the remaining solo piano works

---

*Eventually this boxed set was rereleased as two separate discs and, at the same time, the remaining songs were issued as a third record. These were sung almost entirely by Helen Vanni, but one selection required a baritone voice, and Glenn enlisted the aid of a vocalist living in Toronto named Cornelis Opthof. We recorded his contribution early on when we began working in Eaton's Auditorium. Mr. Opthof was a pleasant chap with a fine voice, but he was obviously not prepared for the intense work atmosphere generated by a typical Gould session. Glenn was used to being the only one performing and, as such, could literally dictate the timing of work periods and rest periods. Sometimes the former could be quite extended until enough material had been recorded to warrant a "rest"—actually, a playback session of the key takes just performed.

I recall that the work on the baritone song was going on at some length and, through the microphones, I could hear occasional panting and deep breathing from the vocalist. Soon, completely exhausted and out of breath, Opthof pleaded: "Pardon me, but could we rest for a minute?" Glenn's answer was solicitous, courteous, and immediate: "Why, of course!"

There was now a dead silence in the auditorium and I suddenly became aware of the silent ticking of Gould's internal clock. Sure enough, after sixty seconds had elapsed, the air was broken by Gould's cheery voice: "Good! Now, let's continue with the passage at the top of page three!"

so that the two-record set could be released. It was not until all of this "Trial by Schönberg Fire" was over that we got the chance to record some conventional music together.

The new project was the *Emperor* Concerto of Beethoven, and the orchestra was going to be the American Symphony conducted by Leopold Stokowski. I was filled with pride and excitement that I was going to be allowed to produce this important recording. To understand fully the emotional impact of the situation, one must learn a little about the inner workings of the Masterworks Department.

At the time I joined as Music Editor (the title for the position that was the first rung on the ladder that would eventually lead to Producer), the departmental staff consisted of the Director of Masterworks—John McClure; three producers—Tom Frost, Tom Shepard, and Paul Myers; one Associate Producer—Richard Killough; and one Music Editor—myself. Now, in those halcyon days of the recording business, it was possible for a company the size of Columbia Records to maintain on its artists' roster more than one exclusively contracted symphony orchestra. In fact, Masterworks boasted three: the New York Philharmonic, the Philadelphia Orchestra, and the Cleveland Orchestra. These three plums were the envy of the producing staff as they represented recordings with the most interest and prestige, and every newcomer to the department aspired to the day when he too might produce the recordings of an orchestra.

John McClure produced the New York Philharmonic with the assistance of Killough as his editor. Sometimes Shepard substituted for McClure when the latter's duties as department head prevented him from directing the sessions. Tom Frost produced the Philadelphia Orchestra with me recently hired to be his editor and, on a few occasions, his substitute. Paul Myers worked with the Cleveland Orchestra and really had no assistant—principally because the Cleveland recorded less than the other two orchestras and because Paul's other duties were not as time-consuming as McClure's and Frost's.

If a project materialized that involved an orchestra other than the above three, it was usually assigned to one of the producers just mentioned. Clearly, the prospect of my working with an orchestra, even for one disc only, was a very exciting one for me, especially as I was only in my first year with the Masterworks Department.

The *Emperor* sessions went without much incident, but I do remember that we nearly got off to a bad start. Strangely enough, the fear that was in our minds concerning this potentially volatile collaboration never actually materialized. Gould, of course, was well known for his unconventional interpretations and tempos. Stokowski was not exactly innocent in this same regard, so it was with some trepidation that we placed these two strong personalities in the studio together to make music. Partly it was luck that it did not blow up, but it was not altogether simply good fortune. I think that Glenn truly idolized Stokowski, who was fifty years his senior, and therefore was perhaps a little more deferential than he had been known to be in the past (and the future, for that matter).

One of the skeletons rattling around in the vaults of Columbia Records was an aborted set of recordings of the *Ophelia Lieder,* opus 67 of Richard Strauss. Just a matter of weeks before the recording of the *Emperor,* Glenn and Elisabeth Schwarzkopf had to terminate their projected recording schedule due to "differences of opinion." I wasn't there, but Paul Myers later confided to me that Glenn had very strong ideas about the way the Strauss songs should be performed (not any less strong than his ideas concerning the Schönberg *Lieder*) and little by little started to "teach" them to Miss Schwarzkopf. This approach was not unlike what I saw take place at the Vanni sessions. One small factor made the difference, however: Helen

Vanni was willing to be "taught" by Gould and Elisabeth Schwarzkopf was not. So, with the smoldering remains of the Schwarzkopf sessions still fresh in our noses, we were legitimately concerned about the Stokowski collaboration. However, the event that nearly got us off to a bad start had nothing to do with personality clashes.

Gould had already made his bold move to give up concertizing two years previous to the *Emperor* sessions, so we all knew that no public performance was going to precede the recording. Because of this, a generous amount of recording time was allowed for the project so that the American Symphony could be rehearsed on the spot and all other matters of interpretation could be ironed out. So when the sessions began, we in the control room utilized the ensuing rehearsal for the much-needed purpose of setting the balances of our microphones. The cost of orchestral recording was staggering, even in those days, so it was really a luxury to use extended passages for balancing as opposed to the quick snatches of orchestral texture that are usually provided for this purpose. After the first runthrough, I felt we were ready to make an official take. What I was not ready for was the question that Gould asked over the microphones at the conclusion of the rehearsal: "Can I come in and hear some of that?" Obviously he assumed we had been taping as they practiced. But, in fact, we had not. In a valiant attempt to keep my voice from sounding as if it were still in the adolescent process of changing, I announced over the talk-back system that we had not been taping. *"What!!?"* shouted Gould. "All my important solos were covered in that performance!"* I bravely mumbled something about being sure that we had never agreed to tape rehearsals but that that

---

*"Covered," in recording lingo, means that an acceptable performance of a particular passage has been committed to tape at least once. "Not covered" are often the last two words a producer utters between the time he listens back to the tapes the next day (when the orchestra has long since been dismissed) and the hour he chooses to take his own life.

lack would never happen again, and we were back to work. Naturally, from that moment to the end of the project, if someone in the studio so much as whistled a recognizable tune, our machines were rolling. Of course, in conformity with all the laws of statistics, no part of these rehearsal recordings was ever pressed into service when the final editing took place.

After Glenn and I had gone over the tapes to devise an editing plan, and after the actual splicing had been completed but before the final mixing of the three-track master into a two-track tape suitable for cutting the disc, we became aware that Stokowski wanted to do the mixing himself—that is, he wanted to be the one who instructed the engineer in the musical adjustment of the track levels. Stoky had quite a reputation around the halls of the Columbia Records Studios in regard to the question of mixing.

An oft-told story relates how he had—in the preparation of another record—wanted to do the mixing himself (this time I mean with his hands actually on the controls), but was told that union regulations prohibited anyone but a registered member from touching the equipment. His insistency, plus the ingenuity of some mediating executive, gave birth to a bizarre but novel scheme. The union engineer actually manipulated the controls, but Stokowski's fingers rode "piggyback" above the engineer's and, by prodding and scratching, caused the latter's fingers to move as surrogates of his own.

Well, the intervening years had taught Stoky that that kind of trick wouldn't work anymore, but he still wanted to be the one to supervise the engineer in place of the producer. Now, it must be understood that adjusting the track levels for musical balances is not the only activity that goes on in the process called "mixing." Numerous technical operations must occur along with the musical ones, and it was at once clear that Stokowski would have neither the patience nor the expertise to perform these tasks. Therefore, it was evident to us that he would not be able to perform the full mixing operation in a satisfactory manner. However, I also realized that keeping track of his preferences about orchestral balances would certainly be a help to me when the real mixing was undertaken. So, it was decided to have Stoky come in, participate in an ersatz mixing session, do his post-facto conducting, and then we would discard the achieved results in favor of a more careful and complete job. I intended discreetly to keep my own set of notes as I observed him in action so that I could retain the essence of his musical judgment while being able to tend to the technical matters when I redid the job.

The plan was carried off per schedule, and my guesses about Stokowski's limited patience were vindicated when I saw the system he devised to perform his "mix." Naturally, it is necessary to listen through the raw, unmixed tape at least once in order to construct a mixing plan that will perfect—or, if appropriate—leave alone the musical balances already contained therein. Stoky realized this, and duly auditioned the first movement before he performed his corrections. With a kind of sigh, he repeated his pre-listening process for the second movement. But when it came time for the third movement, his patience had run out and he instructed the engineer that he would dive in and mix it right off the bat. Well, this never could have yielded an acceptable result because if the producer (or even the surrogate producer) signals the engineer when he hears a balance that needs improving, obviously all his cues would be given late; the initial onset of the material would be in bad balance until the correction was performed. None of this seemed to concern Stokowski and, I must say, none of it concerned me that day because I knew that the whole exercise was nothing more than a rehearsal for the four or five days that I was going to spend in carefully planning and performing the proper mixing operation. I had, however, been true to my plan to keep notes as Stokowski progressed and I was able to incorporate all his ideas into the finished record. Needless to say, he never knew that his "mix" was not used. I still treasure the tape of his efforts as a souvenir of the occasion.

I cannot deny that it was a particular thrill working with Stokowski. While he no doubt would have provided us all with a more dazzling experience had we collaborated with him thirty years earlier (which, whimsically speaking, would have found me barely toilet-trained and Glenn as a toddler of four), there were still little glimpses of the old Stoky available for us to see from time to time.

After one of our editing sessions, as he was starting to put on his coat, somehow the subject of marriage came up. With a little twinkle in his eye but with a completely straight face, he informed us in his characteristically clipped Charlie Chan–like accent: "I was married once. Didn't like it. Much better now. Can come home any hour of the day or night . . . drunk or sober. . . ." I had to keep reminding myself: "This man is eighty-four years old!"

Photographs of the two musicians together were taken for use on the album cover, and, predictably, Stokowski demanded complete approval of the picture we used. A very careful perusal of the originals were undertaken and a particularly good pose of them both was enlarged and submitted for Stoky's examination. He didn't like it. Eventually a group of alternates was shown to him, but he would approve only one. Unfortunately, when we examined his choice, we were a bit stunned to see that although Gould was looking straight at the observer, Stokowski had his head turned and was staring away from Gould, right out of the picture—not exactly the ideal portrait of two "collaborators"! Moreover, he demanded that a retouching job be done. Only then did we begin to understand his strange choice. The original photo showed the bags under his eyes, whereas the semiprofile did not reveal this very natural sign of his age. Stokowski, at eighty-four, was still vain! By the time the retouching artist had completed his work, Stoky's portrait was more like a kind of impressionistic oil painting. He loved it.

Incidentally, the original photo was eventually used in a most inventive way. It was a good photo of Glenn, so when his next album was released (the opus 13 and 14 Beethoven sonatas), the retouching artist removed Stokowski from the photograph altogether and Gould was left alone.

Not long after this sonata record (which included the popular *Pathetique*) was completed, the executives at the Columbia Record Club (a large mail-order operation that functioned quite autonomously from Masterworks) felt that we should consider recording the other two of the very popular Beethoven sonatas (the *Moonlight* and the *Appassionata*). They would be willing to release these recordings along with the *Pathetique* as a special record available only to their subscribers. Such an offer was never to be taken lightly because a Columbia Record Club release guaranteed a large sale for an album in addition to what could be garnered in the stores as a conventional retail product.

Glenn, never oblivious to the business side of his record making, readily agreed to the project. This is not to imply that he would have participated in any money-making plan, but these were works that he was going to record eventually in any case. The club was merely requesting a reordering of priorities. So, we began the *Moonlight* and *Appassionata* project. The sessions for the former went rather efficiently and produced a very charming reading with a Finale dazzlingly played at breakneck speed. The latter, however, offered some problems.

To begin with, Glenn announced that he could not tolerate the composition. He simply felt it was bad Beethoven and, for the life of him, was not able to fathom how it had reached a position of such popularity. However, it *was* one of the thirty-two sonatas and, as such, had to be on his long-term schedule for recording. He felt that somehow he would get through it, but requested that he be given the opportunity to write the liner notes himself so that his feelings about the piece could be explained. In fact, he did write this essay, and the whole package stands as one of the most unusual cases in the history of classical records: an artist explaining that he detests the piece recorded therein.

Certain critics felt that his distaste for the *Appassionata* need not have been expressed in print—it was quite obvious from his performance. In the first movement Glenn adopted a basic tempo that was—to be kind—slow. I was curious just how slow it was compared to more conventional interpretations so I conducted the following experiment: I took Rudolf Serkin's recording of the same piece and copied onto tape a bit of the first movement. Then I taped the same section from Gould's performance, but I played his recording at twice the proper speed as I did so. Finally I spliced together the normal Serkin recording with the speeded-up Gould recording. Of course, at the point of the splice, the pitch of Gould's performance jumps up one octave, but the tempo matched Serkin's perfectly! This meant that Glenn had been playing the first movement exactly at half speed. His entire *Appassionata* barely fits on one side of a long-playing record because of its protracted length. Normally the piece lasts about twenty-four minutes; in the Gould recording, it takes thirty-one-and-one-half minutes. Subsequent to the Columbia Record Club issue, this unusual performance was released to the retail market, where the critics had a field day.

Soon thereafter we embarked on a kind of novelty. Glenn had discovered that Franz Liszt had made piano transcriptions of the Beethoven symphonies, and it didn't take long for all of us to agree that it would be a most interesting addition to our catalog if he were to record Beethoven's Fifth Symphony on the piano. The project was nicknamed BL5 (Beethoven-Liszt-5th), and we dove into it with great enthusiasm. Of course, it was not enough for Glenn to be the first to record this long-forgotten transcription, he had to leave his personal interpretive imprint on it as well. So, two unusual things emerged from his performance.

First, there was the matter of the slow movement. The lay public is almost universally under the impression that playing a virtuosically fast passage is a difficult feat, and slow music is much easier. Any seasoned performing artist will explain that playing both very fast and very slow pose tasks of equal difficulty. True, the challenge of cleanly articulating a zillion notes per second is not present when playing a slow passage, but in its place grows the problem of sustaining musical tension, form, and interest. Gould had long since proved that he was a master of rapid passagework, so it seemed that once in a while, he set himself the challenge of seeing how slowly he could play a piece. It was almost as if Glenn had occasionally to flex his "slow" muscles, just to prove he was able to master that end of the tempo spectrum as well. My feeling is that when taken to the extremes that he often exercised, his tempo experiments had a success rate of about 50 percent. In the case of the BL5 slow movement, the performance was plausible, but noticeably slower than conventional interpretations.

Of greater interest was the tempo situation in the third movement. In almost all orchestral performances, the famous Trio, with its robust low-string opening, is played in a slower, somewhat lugubrious, manner compared with the opening of the movement, but Beethoven himself did not indicate in the music that any such tempo slackening should occur. Prompted by this fact, Glenn decided to honor the composer's instructions (perhaps for the first time in quite a while) and play the movement at one consistent tempo. There are two ways in which this could be accomplished. If the whole piece were taken at the speed normally associated with the opening, the Trio would be propelled at an unplayable velocity. So, the mountain had to come to Muhammad: The opening of the movement was slowed down to match the pace at which the Trio was performed conventionally. Making this tempo "work" proved to be a very interesting exercise, and Gould imbued the section with a kind of grotesque, spidery mystery—one of the examples of his control of slow music working to perfection.

In the fourth movement, we encountered for the first time the need to employ a little mechanical trickery. Liszt was renowned for his propensity to write fiendishly difficult technical passages for the piano and, in the process of squeezing Beethoven's orchestration into the range of notes feasibly playable by ten fingers, he spared no demands on the performer's virtuosity. If any pianist was up to the challenge, Gould was, but he pointed to a place in the Finale and explained that while it was barely possible to play what Liszt had written, to do so would turn the performance into a don't-complain-if-the-musical-lines-are-a-little-bit-shaky-because-you-should-be-thankful-that-you're-hearing-all-the-notes-in-the-first-place situation. He felt that if he was allowed to use four hands (by electronically overdubbing one performance on top of another), he could make the section more musical. So, in two or three places in the last pages of BL5, the astute listener can perhaps detect the results of a four-handed performance.

This process worked so well that when Gould subsequently recorded his own transcriptions of Wagner orchestral pieces, he intentionally built into his arrangement a few places (especially in the concluding pages of the *Meistersinger* Overture) where the performer must use "four hands." While this would tend to discourage any other pianist from considering a public performance of the piece, this negative aspect of his arrangement probably never occurred to Gould because he had long since given up live performances himself and this one recording of his transcriptions was undoubtedly the only contact he would ever have with them. Some uninformed writers have speculated that this kind of "black magic" took place in Gould's recording sessions on a regular basis. To the best of my knowledge, the two cited examples constitute the only times that overdubbing was utilized on any of his releases.

I have always found it interesting that over the years so much has been written about Gould's working methods, but, strangely enough, the authors of these revelations had never been in attendance when Gould recorded and therefore could not have the slightest idea what they were writing about. A typical Gould session was protected with a kind of airtight security to keep away outsiders. The usual cast of characters in New York consisted of Gould, a piano tuner, two recording engineers (one to run the recording console; one to run the tape recorders), a security guard, an air-conditioning engineer, an equipment-maintenance engineer, and myself—a total of eight people. In Toronto, the freedom from union regulations allowed the group to be reduced somewhat. There the *dramatis personae* consisted of Gould, a piano tuner (almost always Verne Edquist), a night watchman employed by the building management, and myself (functioning as the two recording engineers, the maintenance man, and, of course, the record producer)—a total of four people.

In both locations, the rule was the same: NO VISITORS. In view of these circumstances, it always amazes me that these writers and critics have had the gall to "report" on the workings of a Glenn Gould recording session. Who could have told them? Certainly I didn't, I don't believe Verne Edquist ever did, and Glenn's own comments (for publication) were carefully laundered so as to avoid details.

Like everything else, I suppose, mysterious and romantic legends spring up about "the Unknown." Lots of people eat that up and writers are always prepared to feed them. In the press, Gould became known as a "tape wizard"; he wasn't. He merely understood the full potential of the tape-splicing process. His recording sessions became publicized as kind of laboratory experiments wherein

Frankenstein monsters were assembled from scraps of carnage; they weren't. All that a visitor might see would be Gould hard at work recording his own interpretation of a piece of music in as accurate and beautiful a fashion as possible. The process was so simple as to be boring to an observer. It consisted of three steps:

1. Record a complete take of the movement (or, in the case of longer works, a large section of the piece).
2. Listen to it and carefully note any finger slips and/or musical balances that were not perfect.
3. Go back to the piano and record small inserts that would fix the errors.

That's all there was.

Now, sometimes there were complications to each of these steps. The quest for the "perfect" basic take could lead to as little as one playing or as many as a dozen attempts or, in rare cases, the realization that success would not be forthcoming that day and that more thought was necessary. Generally speaking, with Bach works, the basic take would be recorded very quickly, for it seemed that Gould had a more stable notion of exactly how a Bach piece was going to go before he even started to play. Mozart sonatas and Beethoven slow movements apparently possessed an elusive quality (at least as far as the interpretation Gould desired was concerned) that sometimes led to copious runthroughs surmounted by the ever-present threat that none of them would qualify at all.

In all the other repertoire (of all Gould's seventy-five or so records, only nineteen contained music by composers other than Bach, Beethoven, Mozart, and Schönberg, and only four contained music not by German or Austrian composers) there did not seem to be any basic interpretive problem. Perhaps Gould's oft-publicized statement that "the only reason to record it is to do it differently" explains why there might have been a direct relationship between the popularity of a particular composition and the difficulty in finding a unique approach. One doesn't have to labor all night, for instance, to come up with a rendition of the piano works of Sibelius that is different from the rather sparse competition. Only once was I aware that Glenn actually had committed to disc an interpretation that was intentionally distorted. It was in the first movement of the Mozart Sonata K. 331, where he adopted a tempo that was painfully slow. So slow, I felt, that all sense of the flow of the piece had been lost. My feelings were confirmed by Glenn's comment at the conclusion of the first take: "There! That'll bug the critics!" It was the only instant in which I saw such a flash of determined perversity. Reviewers constantly accused him of this kind of willful distortion for its own sake, but unless he was really able to keep a secret from me, I believe that he sincerely stood behind all his readings. Of course, the listener had to be of a particularly democratic sort. More than once I came to the realization that my ignorance of some of the repertoire he played made me an *ideal* producer for him because, in these cases, I arrived at the recording session without *any* preconceived notion about how the piece should go. Naturally, I couldn't help but make my own value judgment as I heard him play— fully realizing that the chances were much better than fifty-fifty that what I was hearing was a performance nothing like that which the composer intended. So I tried to answer for myself the simple question: Is this reading musically interesting? With only the one notable exception, I always was persuaded by his "re-composition." If the interpretation made sense in and of itself, I would be guilty of a kind of closed-mindedness to dismiss it out of hand *just* because it was not played in the traditional way. There certainly were any number of places the listener could go to get a conventional recording of Mozart or Beethoven, and Gould's audience soon came to understand that if they bought his recordings, they could expect some interpretive surprises.

But as soon as his performance was committed to disc,

the chapter was closed. He had made his statement and he seemed to have no further interest in the piece. In his profession, this is a rare attitude indeed. Glenn's activity in the field of recording spanned twenty-seven years, and it is remarkable to observe that only twice during this period did he reexamine a piece that he had previously recorded. Gould's fifth recording (released in 1958) included Mozart's Piano Sonata K. 330. This piece was recorded again by him as part of volume 3 (released in 1972) of the complete set of sonatas. The most ambitious and significant of these re-recordings was the 1982 version of the *Goldberg Variations,* the piece that virtually launched his career in 1955. For completeness, it should be noted that two fugues from the second book of *The Well-tempered Clavier* were used as fillers in his 1957 recording of Bach Partitas and, of course, were eventually remade in stereo for the complete *WTC.* Other than these exceptions, he functioned as a recording artist for nearly three decades without any desire to revisit old repertoire. In a similar period of time, it would not be unusual to find a popular symphony conductor working on his third recording of the complete Beethoven symphonies.

During the actual taping process, Glenn offered all his production teams a built-in problem. It is proper studio decorum for the performing artist to remain silent for a few seconds at the conclusion of each take. This allows for a certain amount of flexibility in the postproduction process. Most often it is necessary to make a "fade" at the conclusion of the selection, and this is done most smoothly if the only sound remaining at the end of a performance is what is known as "room tone." It is a little difficult to explain why this silence is described as a "sound," but in fact it is—a very quiet sort of low-level "bubbling" noise that is what you would actually hear in a "quiet" room if you could turn up the volume control on your ears. Ears are quite marvelous devices and although one's first impression is that, unaided, this room sound is inaudible, in fact, if it is abruptly turned off, the sudden lack of it becomes instantly obvious.

When a musical selection has concluded and all that is left is the room tone, there still remains the problem of gracefully exiting from that sound as well. There exist three choices: (1) Don't terminate the room tone and have it link directly to the next musical selection; (2) splice the room sound directly to leader tape (a paper or plastic tape that is completely silent and is used to separate musical selections), but this is the least satisfactory method for it creates the very noticeable "sudden-cessation" effect noted above; (3) make a fade (a gradual reduction in volume that eventually culminates in complete silence). Even though this concluding fade spreads out over only a second or two, it is always perceived as a superior way of exiting from the room sound and joining to leader tape.

For reasons best known to himself, Glenn persisted in beginning his spoken post-take self-critique so close to the end of the final note that, almost every time, the reverberation in the studio or auditorium had not yet died into inaudibility. Later, the final mixing process would find us spending hours practicing unnaturally fast fades that were designed to taper off the reverberation into silence before the air was broken by Glenn's voice telling us that the take was "super" or "classy" or not yet "bang on." All the reader has to do is listen to some of Gould's very early recordings and a festival of abrupt hall-sound changes will parade themselves before his ears.

Of course every producer tried to get him to stop these premature interruptions, but nothing seemed effective. One day an interesting plan occurred to me. I realized that an overwhelming number of these "short tails" took place between movements (the remainder occurred during the final moments of a complete selection). I explained to Glenn that it would be much easier for me to do the editing if he were to specify the proper duration of the pauses between movements. Doing so would require him actually to "time out" the silence before the next movement commenced and then start to play the new material. Naturally, in the finished master, this abortive opening would be replaced by the properly edited version, but the actual time of its inception would have been premarked on the tape by Gould's own taste. Having exact control over these "musical silences" must have appealed to him, because he adopted the scheme from that day forward.

The fact is that I hadn't lied: The "marking" of these new entrances really was a help. However, what I didn't tell him was that while he was engaged in "feeling" the proper moment for the new movement to begin, he wasn't talking. This didn't solve all of Glenn's early interruptions, but it certainly made an enormous improvement in the vast majority of them.

In addition to this kind of problem intruding into the recording process, it must be noted that the listening process could sometimes take more time than the taping itself, especially if the basic take could be committed to tape in a relatively few tries. Usually, Glenn knew when he came into the control room which take he thought would act as the skeleton of the piece. Sometimes he would ask for a playback of the last two attempts, but unless we were going to be involved in one of those rare, endless searches, the choice was made quickly.

Now, choosing the basic take was only part of the listening task. The performance then had to be subjected to the most minute scrutiny to weed out any and all imperfections. These were noted by both Glenn and myself so that step three, the repairing of them, could run smoothly. It was not unusual for the basic take (let us say of a five-minute movement) to occupy only fifteen minutes of recording time before it revealed itself. However, analyzing it and marking all areas of insufficiency could easily take an additional forty-five minutes.

• • •

These post-take listening sessions were also an opportunity for Glenn to partake of a cup of coffee. During the period we were recording in New York, there was always someone available to go out and bring in refreshments, or they could be delivered by the merchant. But in Toronto, two factors tended to change that procedure. First, as we were recording in the evening almost exclusively, the choices of coffeeshops that remained open were few. Second, the reduced size of our recording team limited the flexibility of this *routine*. This word is carefully chosen; for Gould, everything had a routine. It was almost as if the constant repetition of certain rituals created a kind of security blanket. It went like this: Verne Edquist —who willingly inherited this job out of friendship— would leave the building and go to a nearby all-night coffeeshop. He was usually free to do this during actual recording periods because his real job, keeping the piano in tune, occupied him only before the session began and during playback breaks. Glenn would usually signal at some point during recording that it was time for Verne to embark on his quest so that he could return, beverages in hand, by the start of the listening period.

Early on, Glenn had determined that he liked his coffee best with two sugars and extra cream. This beverage was quickly named a "double-double," and from that moment on it was almost never referred to as coffee. At the appropriate point in the session, we would hear: "Verne, would you like to go out and get some double-doubles?" I had always believed that Gould had invented the name and was quite surprised to hear the term used quite recently in the dialogue of some television show. Of course, this incident is not conclusive proof that Gould had not coined the expression; nor do I believe that although television scripts can be influenced by many factors, the search for coffee at 2:00 A.M. in downtown Toronto is one of them. Most probably, the world simply recognized a good thing when it saw it.

•   •   •

In order fully to understand the technique of taping inserts to fix errors, it is necessary to delve a little more deeply into the basic recording process. The procedure I am about to describe really didn't reach full flower until our operation moved to Toronto. There we were able to concoct almost any recording scheme we desired without worrying about union complications and personnel limitations. During the actual recording, four separate tape machines were running. First there were the two Ampex AG-440 stereo machines that recorded at 15 ips (inches per second) with Dolby A noise reduction units. These were the tapes that would be taken back to New York, edited, and become the masters for disc cutting. Then there was a Sony machine that recorded at 7½ ips (non Dolby). These tapes stayed in Toronto so that Glenn could listen to the results of the sessions and devise a definitive editing plan. Finally there was an old Ampex mono machine that recorded a temporary tape to be used while inserts were made.

The unique feature of this step, which set Gould's recording process apart from that of any other artist I have ever worked with, was Glenn's obsessive concern with whether the inserts about to be recorded would match the selected basic take and the extreme lengths we went to in order to assure that match. Needless to say, if all the recording for a particular piece was done in one session, then the technical parameters of microphone placement and balance automatically would be consistent throughout the process. What was of prime concern, however, was the question of musical performance variation. Initially, this focused on the question of tempo. We realized that the only safe method of ensuring that the speed of the insert would be the same as the basic take would involve playing back the original take to Glenn, seated at the piano (not just any representative sample, but the bars immediately preceding the point where the insert was needed), and then, with a minimum loss of time (so as to avoid any error due to memory slippage), recording the insert itself.

Obviously, the sample of the basic take that would be used for this playback demonstration could not come from the essential Dolby tapes because to do so would introduce an enormous delay while the tape was fast-forwarded from the vicinity of the defect to an area of blank tape so that recording could commence. Then imagine the nightmare if repeated attempts at the insert were required! We would have to shuttle back to the basic take for tempo verification, then shuttle forward again to locate the next available area of blank tape.

To make this "comparison" method feasible, the fourth recorder was used. It was cued up to play back the required lead-in material, the other three recorders were started, the playback tape was begun and fed out to the studio over our normal communication speaker, and finally, when the lead-in material had reached the appropriate point in the music, the playback tape was stopped, a take identification number was "slated," and Gould would begin to record the insert. All of this may sound a bit complicated, but we had it down to a science and, in full swing, the system operated smoothly and efficiently.

After several years of recording in Toronto, functioning as I have just described, Gould began to become concerned over whether the inserts were going to match in volume as well as tempo. Please understand that this concern was not because we had been "burned" on previous occasions in the areas of tempo and dynamics. Quite the contrary, all the years that we worked in New York were done without the split-second switchover from listening to recording, and I really cannot remember any instances when a tempo or level discrepancy disqualified a planned splice repair. Nonetheless, after we had become expert in tempo matching, Glenn added the wrinkle that I had to write down the reading from the recorder meters when the imperfect spot in the basic take was reached and then I had to watch the meters again during the insert process and see if he was playing at the same intensity level. Considering the number of tasks I had already undertaken to perform, I didn't exactly relish this new one. Many times I was not able to wheel around fast enough to read the meters when we recorded the inserts (the tape machines were positioned to my left, not directly in front). I began to feel like one of those one-man bands with contraptions positioned near every available appendage! I had to start the machines, cue up the playback tape, watch the score so that the crossover point in the music was not passed, execute the crossover, keep a written log of the takes recorded, read the score as he recorded so I could answer questions about what he had just done, and now—he wanted me to read the meters also! It got just a bit touch and go.

A typical recording session in Toronto would start at about 7:00 P.M. and sometimes go as late as 1:00 A.M. or 2:00 A.M. There would really be no break for me in this stretch of six or seven hours. Glenn, of course, would alternate recording and listening so I'm sure he felt that he was experiencing both work and rest periods. However, I was confined to my chair continuously for the entire session. It was hard work. Usually we would record for only two nights, rarely three, and then I would pour myself onto a plane and return to New York.

Once safely home, the next phase of the operation could begin: the editing process. First, I must explain that there was not necessarily a correspondence between the compositions just recorded and the ones to be edited next. The order in which Columbia Masterworks decided to release Gould's records determined the order in which the pieces were edited. There was always some recording up for editing at any given moment, and it mattered little whether the work was the product of our most recent recording activity or of some previous session. To keep on schedule, all that had to be done was to supply finished tapes in time for the release date.

The process would start in Toronto with Glenn listening to the "Sony copies" of a particular session and then drawing up an exact splicing plan; that is, a detailed schedule of what parts of what takes were to be spliced together to yield the finished performance that would appear on the record. Generally Gould marked this plan in the score itself, using dividing lines and take numbers to show its makeup.

When Glenn had finished this bit of work, we would confer by phone. Initially he would call me, but after a while we discussed the fact that the process of choosing the takes was really producer's work (although no one but Gould himself could perform this task) and therefore his involvement in the job was actually saving Columbia money, so it seemed like a lot to ask to have Glenn pay for the lengthy international call himself. Therefore, it was decided that he would place a brief call to me in order to indicate that he had completed the editing plan. Then I would call him (using my CBS telephone credit card) so he could transmit the plan over the phone.

Most of Gould's long telephone conversations with me took place between the hours of 11:00 P.M. and 1:00 A.M.— sometimes for the entire two hours. In addition, as I think back, I can't remember a time when he began a conversation with the polite question: "Can you talk now?" The phone rang, he was on, and I was stuck. I invented a little hand signal to give to my wife. It was an imitation of the letter *G* that I made with my thumb and first finger. I signaled it twice—*GG*—and this meant it was going to be a long, long telephone call.

The task at hand was merely to get me to write in my score the same editing instructions that he had inscribed in his. For compositions of moderate length, this process should not have taken an hour, but Glenn accompanied each splicing instruction with an anecdote or supporting reasoning—really not always necessary for the rather mechanical job of splicing tapes together.

Sometimes Glenn would be surprised by what he found when he did his listening. "You know how we thought that take six was the basic take? Well, when I listened carefully, I found that take five is much more interesting for the first page of the movement. Of course, take five has different mistakes in it than take six, but we should be able to fix those with a combination of using take six and its associated inserts." So, sometimes the carefully planned, tempo-matched, volume-matched (growl) scheme that had been devised in Toronto would be discarded temporarily in favor of an ad hoc affair that would carry with it the same insecurities of editing success that every other pianist risks in his recordings. But at least Glenn knew his fallback position. The worst that could happen (if some of these last-minute-inspiration edits failed) was that we could revert to the original plan.

After the editing instructions were meticulously inscribed in my score—and my life suitably enriched by stories, speculations, and other bits of humorous Canadiana—the burden now fell to me to do the actual splicing. Here was where a significant difference existed between recordings made in New York and recordings made in Canada. To understand this, the rules of union jurisdiction must be explained.

Columbia Records ran a union shop in its engineering department. This meant, among other things, that only union engineers were permitted to run the equipment, do the splicing, and make the original recording. This jurisdiction, however, did not extend outside of a five-hundred-mile radius around New York City, nor did it extend beyond the boundaries of the United States. Toronto was exempt on both counts. Therefore, it was perfectly permissible to make the recordings up there using any facility we chose with any personnel we chose. Also, the splicing of the tape could be done in Toronto, similarly unencumbered by union restrictions.

On the other hand, recordings made in the New York studios by union personnel could be spliced only by members of the union under the direction, of course, of the producer. Gould's choosing of the takes was permissible either way. He used copies of the original tapes so it was not "illegal" for him to pore over these tapes himself. Then, in either case, he had to phone me the plan. If it was for a New York recording, I would then book official editing time in the engineering building and work with a union engineer to do the splicing. If it was for a Toronto recording, I did the splicing myself in my own home. This might have been technically against the union contract, but I risked it anyway because of two factors: (1) undoubtedly it would have been completely legal to stay in Toronto to do the splicing; and (2) it was truly impossible for the engineering department to ascertain where the editing was done.

The reasons for splicing at my home were many. First, I could work on my own schedule, day or night. Second, there is no question that the efficiency of the task increases to the point where the length of time to accomplish it is roughly divided by two if a second person is not involved. Third, the Masterworks Department was saved the expense of rather extensive editing time in the Columbia Recording Studios. Yes, the engineering department actually charges the Masterworks Department for the use of its studios and personnel. The fact that *both* departments exist under the common umbrella of Columbia Records does not alter the well-known corporate doctrine: One hand charges the other.

On a personal level, I worked out a financial provision with the head of my own department, which acknowledged the fact that although I would have been required to be present whether I performed the splicing myself or whether I supervised an engineer who did the work, in the former case I was additionally contributing the use of my home studio and equipment. This arrangement proved to be advantageous to Masterworks because it was a flat fee calculated to be only a fraction of what the engineering department would have charged for the same facility.

A humorous sidelight: By the early 1970s, every album released by Columbia Records had inscribed on the liner notes the name of the producer and the names of the two principal engineers, usually the man who did the initial recording and the man responsible for the editing. Well, in the case of the Toronto-born Gould albums, I played the role of both men. So, it seemed only logical that I receive credit as engineer as well as producer. In fact I could easily have done that as union jurisdiction was not violated, but, in reality, I felt it was wiser not to flaunt my Canadian activities in print. However, my own sense of whimsy prompted me to invent two names for the contributing Canadian "engineers," and these names mark every album that emerged from Toronto under the above-described circumstances. The recording technician was Kent Warden. This was a pseudonym I had concocted many years earlier for use in entering contests for musical compositions. *Kent* was a kind of contraction of Kazdin and Fenton (my middle name) and *Warden* was a simple reshuffling of the letters in Andrew. But my real masterpiece was the name of the editing engineer: Frank Dean Dennowitz. This was constructed as a complete anagram of my whole name: Andrew Fenton Kazdin.

Not only was the Columbia engineering staff unaware of these pseudonyms, but so were most of the other employees of the company. Proofreaders, liner-note writers, editors, and other executives had no idea these were fictitious people. After several years of using these names—and referring to these "engineers" as if they really existed—they sort of became household words around certain quarters of Columbia Records. Eventually Frank Dean Dennowitz's activities expanded to encompass two albums recorded in Israel and one record originating in London, England. I still treasure a gift given to me by my daugh-

ter: a T-shirt on which was emblazoned FRANK DEAN DEN-
NOWITZ LIVES. I wore it once to a recording session in
Toronto and displayed it to Gould—one of the few people who was "in" on the joke—whose funny bone was
suitably tickled. My real fantasy was never fulfilled, however. To this day I think I would have treasured above
all else a Grammy Award for Best Engineering given to
Kent and Frank.

After the tapes were spliced together to form a complete
performance, Glenn had to hear the results to determine
whether everything fit in place as he had envisioned it.
The initial approach to this phase of the work was to send
a tape copy to Toronto or, if our schedules should match
in a fortuitous way, play the tape when he was next in
New York. Soon this very cumbersome postal method
(given the fact that we not only had the mail services of
two countries to contend with, but the Canadian Customs
clearance process as well) gave way to what we thought
was a novel improvement. Glenn always had maintained
a close working relationship with the Canadian Broadcasting Company (CBC) in Toronto, and through that
contact discovered that audio tie lines were in existence
that linked the offices of the CBC in Toronto with those
in New York. Furthermore, it was learned that there were
periods during the day that were not particularly busy for
this hookup. So, the plan was devised to have me bring
the tape I wished Glenn to hear over to the CBC New
York office. Then, when transmission activity was at a low
point, they would play back the tape over the tie lines,
and the signal would be recorded by a machine in Toronto. Finally, all that remained was for Gould to drop
by the CBC office near his home and pick up the copy.
Voilà! Audio from New York to Toronto! No mail, no
customs, no high frequencies. However, the essential
message was able to get through: How well did the splices
work?
    Not long after we developed this method, we reached

the final solution. This was not only the most reliable system, but the most convenient for both Glenn and myself. Once again the telephone came to our aid. I constructed a direct phone patch in my home, which allowed me to play back a tape directly into the telephone lines, thereby bypassing the weakest link in the system: the carbon microphone in the handset. Signals thus transmitted sound not nearly as badly as one might guess, and it was soon determined that the quality of sound heard in Toronto was more than sufficient for Gould's purposes. After all, he knew the actual nature of the audio from all the listening sessions in Toronto. All he was interested in at that stage was whether any subtle tempo changes or objectionable volume differences had been created during the splicing. Both types of defects could be heard easily over our phone hookup. And so, for many years, this was the way Gould approved his solo albums.

When it came to recordings involving a collaborator (Bach violin sonatas, Bach gamba sonatas, Hindemith brass sonatas, Hindemith's *Marienleben*), in addition to all the above steps, the question of musical balance between the forces was critical and the telephone-transmission method was insufficient. Glenn had to hear an actual high-quality copy of the final tape to be able to approve it for release. Usually I brought the tape with me when I next went to Toronto for recording, and Glenn would listen to it right then.

Before leaving the subject of splicing, it is worth mentioning an interesting effect. During the telephone session when the spliced tape was being played back for his approval, Gould would be taking notes (written or mental) so that he could ask questions and make observations afterward. Now, although Glenn had previously transmitted his exact splicing plan to me before I started work, both of us realized that not every theorized splice could be made into a viable reality. I used to tell new editors starting work at Columbia that when it came to splicing, there was only *one* thing of which they could be absolutely sure, and that was the fact that they could *never* be sure! The easiest-looking juncture of takes on paper could prove to be completely unworkable when the tape was actually cut; conversely, the most impossible-looking splice might just work when executed. So, Glenn knew that when I played the edited tape to him, even though he had the original plan in front of him as he listened, certain cuts might not have turned out to be exactly on the note he had originally suggested, perhaps taking place a few notes earlier, or later, or even embodying a momentary excursion through a take not included in his plan in order to smooth over a trouble spot.

Of course, if a splice is executed properly, there is no clue left to its existence; a skillfully edited tape should sound seamless. When Glenn listened for the first time to the master tape, he could never be sure whether or not there was actually a splice exactly where his plan indicated one. This fact led to an interesting situation. Many times, after the playback was concluded, he would ask: "Was there a splice two measures before the change of key? You know, I hear it speed up there." Almost universally, if my answer was affirmative, he would ask me to find some other way of conjoining the takes in that general area, but if my answer was negative, he would sort of shrug his shoulders, realize that he had actually played it that way—with a little acceleration—and let it pass. I always found it fascinating that small tempo changes that were unacceptable if caused by a splice were completely acceptable if they were part of his actual performance. I continually wondered if he let the "natural" ones pass because he had really neglected to focus on them when he drew up the original plan, and couldn't admit to not having heard the defect in the first place.

2

After approximately sixteen years of commuting to Manhattan for recording sessions, at his own expense, Glenn informed us that the railroad line that had provided him with direct transportation from Toronto to New York was going to discontinue that particular service. The alternative, he went on, was not at all convenient, and he realized that this problem was going to curtail seriously his recording activities in New York. It was this incident that started us thinking about the feasibility of recording in Toronto.

The first issue to be faced was one of cost. From past experiences, I had learned that certain quirks of corporate accounting actually caused the Masterworks Department to treat the kind of "paper" transfers of charges that went on among various sections of Columbia Records exactly as if real dollars had gone out the door. More to the point, the inverse was also held to be true; dollars out the door were of no more consequence than interde-

out the door were of no more consequence than interdepartmental accounting transfers. I always found this hard to believe, but I was constantly told it was so and here was my chance really to find out. I asked the question directly and was told directly. Yes, it would make *no* difference to the costs of an album if we poured real dollars into a Canadian recording studio or if we continued to pay a similar amount—on paper—to our own engineering department.

Well, that solved point number one, although, at best, this is a kind of myopic thinking. Perhaps the Masterworks Department could not tell any difference financially. If you think about it, all their expenses were "paper" transfers, even the ones involving cash to outside businesses. Masterworks didn't have a big can of money to dip into when they had to settle a bill, they simply authorized the corporation to make payment. But the Columbia Broadcasting System itself was another matter. I'm sure they would have complained if they found out that the alternative to paying this bill to a Canadian studio was to have two internal divisions settle it between themselves—with the money staying "in the family."

Next came the actual question of a studio. Glenn, who of course knew the local recording situation fairly well, told me the sad fact that there was no equipped facility in the Toronto area that would be suitable for legitimate piano recording. In that respect, we were lucky in New York. Columbia's famed 30th Street studio was a converted church and, as such, had the internal volume of space to afford a naturally reverberant hall sound to a solo piano. No such building existed in Toronto, that is, with recording equipment built in. So, our thoughts next turned to the possibility of finding any location at all that might provide the right sound and moving portable recording gear into the place each time we wished to use it. This procedure was not unheard of; most recordings of symphony orchestras are made this way.

Glenn did some quick calculations and came up with

the following astounding proposal: If a location that afforded us the right acoustical environment could be found, then he would personally buy any and all equipment that I would specify, rent the recording location himself, pay whatever expenses necessary to transport the gear, and, in return, charge the Masterworks Department an hourly rate exactly equal to the one they were accustomed to paying to their own engineering department. The generosity of this very attractive-sounding offer can be rationalized only by realizing exactly how strong his desire was to record at home. Sooner or later, he figured, he would amortize the equipment. I'm not so sure he ever did.

After testing several possible locations around the city, we came upon Eaton's Auditorium. Eaton's Department store was the Macy's or Gimbel's of Toronto. It was an enormous building—made even bigger by an annex—and it boasted a full-size auditorium on its top floor. This room was used from time to time for small concerts, recitals, and the like. In fact, as a young man, Glenn himself had played an organ recital there. Now he personally undertook the negotiations for its rental. Because of the noise of elevators and other evidence of bustling customers, it was clear that we could use the hall only when the store was empty. This, in turn, suggested evenings and, more specifically, weekend evenings. Glenn was delighted with the acoustics of the place, not only for the way it sounded on tape but for the way it sounded to him as he sat at the piano and played.

And so it came to pass that Gould bought the following recording equipment:

2   Ampex AG-440-2 tape recorders
3   Neumann U-87 microphones
4   Dolby 360 noise reduction units
2   power amplifiers
3   KLH-5 loudspeakers
Boom stands

Multi-conductor audio cable for connecting the auditorium with our backstage control room

A small mixing console

Assorted small devices

Then there was the matter of a few pieces of custom equipment. I designed a talk-back system that also allowed for playing back tapes to the auditorium proper. I drew up plans for units that permitted the splitting of signals so we could record on several machines at once and also select which recorder we wanted to hear on playback. These devices were built by various people Glenn knew around the CBC. All told, I estimate that he invested around $20,000 (in 1970 dollars) in this venture.

Actually, all of the equipment did not arrive at once, so we had to make do for a little while with less than we had originally planned. Our earliest efforts, for instance, were not Dolby encoded. But before very long everything was in place.

Even though it was quite clear that the Eaton Auditorium was the hall we wanted, there still remained the task of deciding on an exact microphone placement to extract the best that the room could offer. We concluded rather quickly that the stage itself was no place for the piano. Having eliminated that, there was really only one other spot left: the floor of the auditorium right in front of the first row of seats. In fact, the left edge of the piano (from the player's point of view) was almost touching the front lip of the stage.

We made several recording tests this way and although the sound was basically good, Glenn found an unpleasant aspect to it. I tried moving the microphones higher, lower, closer, farther, but nothing alleviated the objectionable quality. As I had to admit that I could not personally hear exactly what was bothering him, we spent long periods discussing it in the hope that with the use of enough words, somehow he could communicate to me what he was sensing. This is perhaps one of the most difficult tasks a producer faces: getting someone who is not conversant with the technical terms that define sound quality to describe definitively his subjective impression when listening to a recording.

In the midst of his attempts, Gould used the word *cluttered* and tried to impart the notion that the various musical lines, or "voices," which he strove to play in a way that gave them independent lives, were somehow "running into each other." Suddenly it occurred to me that perhaps what he was referring to was the acoustic effect created by the small resonant space formed by the body of the piano, the front curved lip, and the lid. We had always recorded in a similar configuration in New York, so I never imagined that the lid could be at fault. In reality, the chief function of the piano lid is to channel and reflect the sound output of the instrument in one direction: horizontally, out toward the audience. In the recording process, this function is unnecessary because microphones can be moved to intercept the direct output of the piano, even if it means putting them in a place that an audience cannot possibly occupy.

So, the lid was removed and the microphones raised somewhat so that they could "look down" on the exposed harp and sounding board. We made another test. Success! As happy as I was to conquer our immediate problem, I was troubled by just one unsolved mystery in this exercise: the fact that the offending resonant space had existed in New York, in the same piano, exactly as we now found it, for several years. Why was it suddenly unacceptable?

For the next nine years this procedure and mike placement was adhered to so strictly that it was possible to record a new insert to fix a blemish heard in a tape made years earlier and have the splice match perfectly. In fact, there were even little crayon marks on the recording console that indicated the level setting of each of the three microphones. Further, marks on the master volume control of the entire console offered the choice of

Bach, Beethoven, and so on. Also, a careful three-dimensional plot that pinpointed the location of each microphone in space was drawn so that the setup always could be reconstructed. I was proud of what I had achieved and didn't want to lose it.

Years later this pride was tarnished with a little bitterness when Glenn himself undertook to produce, for a local label, a recording of another young Canadian pianist using, I'm sure, the very same setup in the very same auditorium. I had long since done all the hard work, and apparently Gould could not see any reason to have me involved (perhaps on a free-lance basis?) in this new commercial record.

This incident leads into a larger issue. On various occasions Glenn was involved in the production of television shows. If he had reacted like most other prominent recording artists, he would have voiced a preference for his "trusted" record producer to be included in the project so as to guarantee the kind of sound he was used to. In the fifteen years that we worked together, only once did he make this kind of gesture (see Appendix 1, p. 170). A track record like that can go a long way toward reinforcing the natural paranoia that goes with being a producer in the record business. After the first few such instances, it began to occur to me that maybe he didn't like our working relationship. But a little man sitting on my other shoulder reminded me that our rapport could not have been bad since we had turned out over twice as many records as all of his other producers combined. Usually the litany of these statistics served to quiet my anxiety, but deep down inside I felt something was peculiar.

My quiescence on the subject was ruffled from time to time by another type of incident. One must remember that although Gould's reputation in the United States was as a sort of eccentric recluse who played brilliantly but sometimes perversely, in Canada he was generally regarded as a kind of national hero. Radio shows, television shows, magazine articles, and newspaper space were devoted to his own creative efforts or to reportage about him. Very frequently I would hear about some magazine or television production wanting to include in their documentary a scene of Gould working on recordings. So, Glenn would happily stage a mock recording session for the cameras, either complete with his own equipment set up in Eaton's, or using an official-looking studio conveniently provided by the CBC. Sometimes it was even necessary to show a producer-type seeming to officiate over the proceedings. Never once was I asked to participate. He would borrow some fellow he knew from the CBC and have him "stand in" for me. Verne Edquist would often tell me about these ersatz sessions and editorialize that it just didn't seem right for some other guy to be getting his picture in a newspaper or on television, when I was the real producer. There were enough of these kinds of opportunities—always arranged to take place when I was not in Toronto—that I began to realize that my absence from his national exposure was not an accident. We never discussed this because I felt that to do so would seem as if I were seeking some self-aggrandizement. Thus I never did find out what was at the root of it all.

I do not believe that the closeness I felt in our relationship was a self-induced illusion. One cannot survive the literally thousands of hours of telephone calls and personal conversations without coming away with the feeling that there was a friendship that transcended the working relationship. In fact, an event from early 1971 reinforces this feeling. We were still in the process of perfecting our "studio" in Eaton's. Many times I would step off a plane from New York, stop long enough in my hotel to drop my bag and phone my wife to confirm my safe arrival, and head straight for Eaton's just in time to find one of the CBC technicians complaining that something was wrong with some of the custom equipment. Rather than relax and prepare myself for the impending session, frequently I had to perform an extensive series of test

42

procedures in order to pinpoint the trouble. These situations reached their peak when I arrived one day and was told that the required cables were not completely constructed. It was clear that, for the good of the recording, I had better chip in and solder a few connectors before Glenn arrived. I was sensitive about losing all chance to compose myself before a long recording ordeal, and I knew I had to somehow put a stop to this last-minute imposition on my time. I thought about how I would broach the subject with Glenn and came to the conclusion that I should write him a note on the matter, rather than sully the atmosphere of our sessions. It read as follows:

Dear Glenn,

As you know, I tend to get ahead of myself sometimes when I talk, so I'm choosing this medium in hopes of clearly expressing my feelings on what I believe to be a rather complicated matter. I'm referring, of course, to certain aspects of our burgeoning studio in Toronto.

At the outset, I must assure you that it is indeed a *situation* and not a *personality* that is the focus of my concern. I have rarely been privileged to meet a man as selflessly devoted to the true meaning of friendship as Lorne Tulk [CBC staff engineer]. His adoration for you and enthusiasm for our project seem limitless and I can think of no way to place a value on them. It is these very qualities which I now find forming the core of a problem.

I arrived in Toronto at 2:30 last week, left the airport at 5:00, checked into my hotel at 5:30, unpacked my bag and (as you pointed out) was in Eaton's well before 6:00. There I found faithful Lorne concluding an entire afternoon of soldering connectors on new patchcords. When he asked if I would assist him, I could not refuse. This task kept me occupied until I discovered the "inadequacies" of John P——'s handiwork. The rest of the evening is history.

I would have appreciated a *few* moments to relax after my trip. Instead, I added the title of "Bench Technician" to the steadily expanding list of my functions. Then, when it was necessary for me to leave on Sunday, I did so with the uneasy feeling that I really should have stayed to help pack up (see subfunction 4B: Stagehand).

Glenn, I'm doing too much. It is telling in my mental and physical fatigue. You must believe that my heart is solidly behind this project, but I must draw the line at some reasonable point. I am perfectly willing to become Project Director, Circuit Designer, Recording Engineer, Maintenance Technician, International Equipment Carrier, and Producer. But the enthusiastic participation of Lorne seems to apply a pressure that I match him "deed for deed." There lies the source of my frustration.

I don't wish to seem like a Prima Donna (on second thought, I don't think there's much chance of hearing that accusation if one compares what I have undertaken to do with what Columbia Records pays me to do) but I must request that some *permanent* steps be taken to relieve me of these duties which I find extraneous, enervating and somewhat demeaning. Perhaps it would be possible to hire those young men that P—— had at Eaton's for our first session. Lifting boxes, pulling dollies, packing speakers, running wires—these are things that could easily be done by these boys.

I'm sure you see the problem. I fear that Lorne's feelings will be hurt if he surmises that his only value exists in "doing the dirty work." Therefore, I find myself "chipping in" to do all sorts of homey functions in order to sort of "prove" to Lorne that there is no prejudice. On the other hand, I am really not capable of doing *everything* that must be done. It is vital that I have complete control over those factors which influence the quality of the product, but this does not mean that I personally elect to lift the speakers as well.

Let's talk about this at greater length when you find it convenient.

At an unpressured moment in our next session, Glenn indeed responded to my note. The bulk of his reply was to assure me that he full well understood my problem and he would see to it that sufficient help was available in the future. However, his opening remarks have always remained in my memory and form the reason for retelling this story here. Glenn explained that although he was in complete agreement with my request, he was somewhat hurt and saddened that this matter had to take the form of a letter. He said he had thought we were close enough friends to make this kind of formality unnecessary. Of course, I assured him that I felt the same way, but I pointed again to my opening sentence and reminded him that I could make a more lucid presentation in print than in conversation. I think he understood.

This whole incident served to etch more sharply the twin thoughts that our friendship was not a figment of my imagination and that I had every right to be bewildered about those moments when he chose to pretend I didn't exist. The concept of an "imaginary" friendship is not so farfetched as it sounds. When an artist/producer association has existed throughout a number of years— through "thick and thin," countless hours of recording and editing, conversations both business and personal—it is quite natural for the elements of true camaraderie to appear. Very often the depth of this relationship can be misread by the producer. This is not to say that the artist is perpetrating a fraud of some kind, but rather merely to indicate that the producer represents to the artist the conduit to his recording career. As such, one might expect a little "artificially deferential" treatment (perhaps better known in the trade as "brown-nosing"). Even when the passage of time has tended to mellow and strengthen the loyalty, my experience has taught me that in the final analysis, at the breaking point, the artist will always put his personal career before the friendship with the producer. Upon consideration, it is clear that it really cannot be any other way. So, there has always been in my mind the possibility that the seemingly apparent elements of friendship are not quite as real as they appear.

A few words should be added here about Lorne Tulk, a CBC staff engineer. I knew about him long before I ever met him. All through the years when Glenn and I recorded in New York, I was fully aware of Gould's activities in Toronto. So involved was he with the CBC that he even had an office there. There were radio concerts and eventually a series of documentaries that Glenn devised, wrote, produced, and edited. In all these endeavors, his favorite engineer was Tulk. The usual pattern was there: Glenn seemed to be involved in Lorne's personal life, including having a warm relationship with Tulk's family; Lorne was the one that Glenn could count on to pull him through some deadline emergency by working long hours; Tulk's dedication was the reason that he helped Gould in the project of bringing the Columbia Records sessions to Toronto. As can be seen by my letter, Lorne worked long and hard in seeing the specially constructed electronic devices through to completion.

A friendship grew between us after several recording sessions, and he expressed a desire to learn more about electronics. He was talented in woodworking as well and designed two cabinets on wheels to hold the large Ampex tape recorders, the Dolby units, and other small devices. He built these units with his own hands and I'm not at all sure what he asked of Glenn in return for his handiwork. He was, however, physically frail and as our project grew, found it unwise to lift and move the heavy equipment.

At this point Lorne introduced us to Ray Roberts who was willing, with the aid of his son, to do the heavy work associated with each recording session. Considering all the other contributions that Lorne had made besides physical ones, it is a little disheartening to contemplate that as soon as his "strong back" gave out, Glenn had no use for him. But viewed in retrospect, that turns out to be an inescapable conclusion. Glenn engineered the cross-fade of Tulk to Roberts—not only professionally, but socially as well—so skillfully that I scarcely was aware it was happening. However, I think Lorne sensed it and, to a certain extent, was relieved because his involvement with Glenn had assumed proportions that threatened to be all-consuming. As I was myself finding out, Gould had a way of practically "swallowing" people in an engulfing kind of friendship/control.

Although his friendship and help were missed, it was possible to carry on without him or a substitute of similar qualifications because by this time in the development of our studio operations, everything was running on track. All the custom-made equipment had been completed and the "bugs" had been worked out of the system.

Ray started as a helper in moving—a kind of stagehand. Although he had no training in music or electronics, he was bright and had certain mechanical talents (first evidenced in his knowledge of automobiles). Soon it became clear that if I drew up a kind of "put tab A into slot B" diagram, Ray could set up the microphones, stands, power supplies, tape recorders, Dolby units, and monitoring equipment and wire them together so that there remained for me only to align the tape machines, check the mike positions, and make level tests. Then we were ready to record. This was an enormous help—just the kind I had pleaded for in my letter to Glenn.

Ray would show up at Eaton's a sufficient number of hours in advance of my scheduled arrival so that everything was prepared by the time I got to the auditorium. Then he would wait around just long enough to see that all the equipment was functioning properly, take his leave, and return at the end of the evening (regardless of the hour) to help pack up. Usually a phone call to warn of our projected wrap-up time was his signal to come back. It got to be standard practice for Ray and me to have a little "shakedown" meeting at the conclusion of the last session of each trip, and this was my opportunity to tell him if anything was in need of servicing before my next visit. Or, during the early days, I could ask him to purchase—on behalf of Glenn Gould Limited—any small devices or tools whose need became apparent as we progressed.

The preceding paragraphs recount the relationship that Ray Roberts had to the recording project, but it became clear that his involvement with Glenn began to take on many other facets. Little by little Ray started to do other tasks for Gould. It probably started with Glenn's car, which Ray understood far better than its owner. Then I observed him being useful in other areas until it became apparent that Glenn was using Ray generally to act as an interface with the outside world. As Glenn drew deeper and deeper into seclusion, Ray did more and more for him. I'm not completely sure, but I would not rule out grocery shopping and laundry from the list of duties. I was never privy to the kind of financial remuneration that Ray received for his services, but it was probably generous.

So dependent did Glenn become upon Ray that when he came to New York, in his last years, he brought Ray Roberts with him. As CBS in New York provided all of the services for which Ray was originally hired in Toronto, I can only assume that Ray functioned for Glenn as a kind of "valet." In fact, at the end, when Glenn realized that he was experiencing a profound physical assault (the stroke that claimed his life), he called only Ray for help. Consider this carefully. Gould's father was still alive. Did Glenn have *no* close friends? There can be no more accurate barometer of the importance Ray Roberts had assumed in Gould's life than to recount this fact. It even seemed that Ray was in charge of Glenn's funeral arrangements.

But, like a tale oft heard before, in a final conversation after Glenn's death Ray revealed to me that he too had sensed the imminent dissolution of their relationship, and his growing observations of the way Gould "used" and discarded other people both prepared him for the inevitable and provided the seeds of disenchantment that made the probable outcome seem a bit more like a relief than a shock.

The revelation of this thought both surprised me (I believed that Ray would remain in Glenn's employ for a much longer time) and started me thinking again about the pattern of these friendships. In addition to the two men—Tulk and Roberts—who had lived through their cycles, there was another person who could always have been counted on to be part of Gould's "camp": his piano tuner.

I don't know exactly how long Verne Edquist tuned pianos for Glenn Gould, but I think it was for years before I met him in Toronto. Verne was a tall, lanky gentleman, who, like so many others in his profession, had extremely poor eyesight—the evidence of which was a pair of glasses with lenses that had a central section built like the proverbial Coke bottle bottom. He came from a region of Canada that imprinted its residents with a vocal accent similar to what we in the United States associate with Maine and Vermont. His speech was peppered with expressions like "By golly!" and I always had the feeling that I was talking to a man at least ten years older than he really was.

His expertise at his craft was complete. In my many years producing piano recording sessions, with a wide variety of piano tuners in attendance, I can say truthfully that I have rarely met his equal and have yet to meet his superior. Gould was extremely lucky to have this man in his service.

After Ray Roberts, Verne was usually the second one to enter the hall. When I arrived, he would be in the final stages of a complete tuning. By the time the actual recording began, his work was mostly complete but his attendance was required throughout the session to ensure against tonal slippage or a more serious accident, like a broken string or other part of the piano's mechanism. So Verne spent most of his time in the control room with me. In fact, he inherited a small job in the actual recording process. Because it was necessary to start four different tape machines every time we began to record, and these recorders were spread around me in a kind of circle, Verne, by manning the Sony unit, made it unnecessary for me to stand up. He made a good companion during the long sessions, being completely quiet when that was appropriate and the purveyor of interesting conversation during those moments when Gould wanted to practice something without the tape running. It was during these chats that I found out about events such as my "stand-in" making another appearance before the cameras. Verne was also devoted to "the cause," and this put him at Glenn's beck and call. His personal time was very often intruded upon by the daily twists in the recording schedule. I think he sensed a kindred spirit in me (in this regard) and felt safe in letting his mild annoyance find expression.

Glenn had a way of periodically causing a person to account for himself. This is a rather difficult concept to describe, but eventually everyone who dealt with him became aware of it. Sometimes it would intrude itself into moments of levity, and just when lighthearted banter would be at its comedic peak, he would freeze the air by saying: "I, uh . . . don't know quite what you mean by that, sir. . . ." Then one had to go through the excruciating task of explaining a joke and proving that there was absolutely nothing derogatory toward him contained therein. Verne was not exactly a master of smooth rhetoric and Glenn's quizzing could easily unsettle him. This was too bad because very often the topic of conversation was the piano. I know that, mentally, Gould had Verne compartmentalized as a tuner only—someone who could tend to the piano as long as nothing serious was wrong, but not an experienced technician who could put right a more formidable problem of regulation. Many times, if a little symptom of trouble presented itself, Verne would try to explain what it was and offer to fix it. By the time Glenn had finished putting him through the verbal wringer, Verne would get so tied up that he sounded not altogether sure of his diagnosis. Gould would then give him the spoken equivalent of a pat on the head and decide to let the problem exist until (this next never spoken, but I felt implied) a "real" technician could look after it. I was never able to find out exactly how proficient Verne actually was in matters other than straight tuning because Glenn never gave him a chance to prove it. However, it was just not practical to keep two piano men on standby during the entire run of the sessions, and I know that neither Glenn nor I would have wanted to settle for any other tuner than Verne. So Verne tuned, and matters of regulation were postponed.

On more than one occasion I asked Verne if he ever considered trying to make his career in New York where, I assured him, he would be able to hold his own against the best of them. Perhaps the idea had occurred to him, but Verne Edquist was a family man, his roots were clearly in Toronto, and the prospect of a move of such magnitude held no attraction for him.

Toward the end of his life, I discovered that Glenn had managed to phase out Verne as well. This caused me considerable sadness because the talent and loyalty of this man would have been nearly impossible to replace. I don't know what Glenn's rationale was; perhaps it was related to the fact that Gould started recording on a Yamaha piano. But that would have been a rather flimsy excuse for their professional separation as Verne had tuned even the harpsichord that Glenn used for the Handel suites, and I can't believe that the Yamaha was more unlike a

Steinway than the harpsichord was. But I guess, for me, the deeper pain came from confronting face to face yet another example of what real lack of loyalty was.

An interesting and complex ritual came into being at the end of each recording trip. As soon as we knew we were completely finished, the following activities were triggered: Ray Roberts & Son began to disassemble and pack up the equipment; Verne Edquist would replace the lid on the piano and then lock it with a special U-shaped piece of heavy iron that "muzzled" the keyboard cover so that it could not be opened by any unauthorized person; I would set about the task of packaging and tying the eight or ten reels of recording tape that were the fruits of our weekend (in preparation for their trip to New York); and Glenn would come into the control room (which under normal circumstances was really the "Green Room" of Eaton's Auditorium) change his shirt, flop down on a couch to unwind, and then start writing checks. First he would pay Verne for that weekend's activities. At some point before leaving, Verne would walk to the couch and tell Glenn how many hours he had worked. Then Glenn would do the necessary multiplication and, if it was too late for public transportation to be running, add cab fare and write Verne a check. This was also the time to reimburse Ray Roberts for any recent expenses incurred. In addition, Glenn would write me a check. This needs a little explanation.

When I made my agreement with Columbia Masterworks to do the editing on Gould's records for a flat fee, a discussion ensued about how actually to pay me for this service. For reasons known only to middle-management executives in a large corporation, it was decided that it wouldn't "look right" if CBS checks were drawn to my order. So the following scheme was devised: I had made a rough estimate that it took about two trips to Canada to record the material that would eventually become a single album. Each time I visited Toronto, Glenn would write me a check for an amount equal to about half of my per-album editing fee. I would keep accurate books at home, noting the amounts that CBS actually owed me and the running total of Glenn's contributions. At the same time, Glenn would submit bills to Masterworks representing his hourly studio charge, his expenses for Verne (it was always customary for Masterworks to pay the piano tuner), and then add a figure for what he called "engineering services"—which was, of course, his contribution to my fee. I sometimes wondered whom we were fooling. As far as Masterworks was concerned, this whole procedure was very much on the up-and-up. In fact, as each new executive assumed the position as head of our department, it was necessary for me to bring him into my confidence and explain the "game." The last thing I ever wanted to see was a discovery and misinterpretation of this cash flow by someone who was not informed. I wasn't ready to jeopardize my position with the Masterworks Department over a few dollars. So Glenn would write me a check as well.

But the writing of this small document proved to be an event of no small complexity for him. In some convoluted psychological way, Glenn reasoned that when he wrote someone a check, he was somehow giving away a piece of himself, which, of course, from a fiscal point of view, he certainly was. But this was something far more amorphous and mystical than that. He felt that the element of luck (meaning "good fortune" not "good gambling") figured in here. Please don't expect this explanation to make sense. It won't because it never did. With Glenn, you just went along and played the game. Gould didn't want to give anyone to whom he owed money an "unlucky check." In all my years commuting to Toronto, I never found out what made a check unlucky. I don't think it had anything to do with the check number, certainly not the amount, probably not the way he signed his name; I just don't know.

What would happen is that Glenn would write out

the check—completely—and then sort of stare at it for a moment. In this split second he would know if the check was lucky or unlucky. In the former case, he would simply present it to the new owner. If, however, he deemed the slip of paper to be unlucky, then he would say something like: "Uhhh. . . . I don't think I like this one. Let me do another." Whereupon he would tuck this first draft away somewhere (I don't believe I ever actually saw it ripped up, as one might suspect) and write out another. If this one passed muster, then the ritual was concluded. I believe that once he had to go to a third draft before the document was sufficiently "lucky" to warrant delivery.

The most bizarre of these incidents occurred one evening after he had given me my check and brought the session to a close. I was safely back in my hotel packing my suitcase for the following morning's trip home, when I got a call from him informing me that what I had in my possession was, in fact, an unlucky check. He apologized profusely and told me that he would drop another one off at the front desk of the hotel for me to pick up as I checked out (no pun) in the morning. Naturally, he extracted all kinds of promises from me that I would on no account (also no pun) cash the unlucky one and, of course, I agreed. This was on January 11, 1976. The reason I know the exact date is because I still have the unlucky check. Likely this is the only known example of someone holding—undeposited—a perfectly good check (from the bank's point of view) as a souvenir.

A little aside here. In contrast to some of us whose names can be misspelled in a variety of exotic ways, there was really only one error that anyone could make to botch Gould's appellation: "Glenn" could be, and often was, incorrectly spelled "Glen." The only remarkable thing about this fact is that when Gould himself wrote a check, or (very rarely) gave an autograph (it was equally traumatic for him to give away a simple signature for fear that it would not be "lucky"), he signed himself "Glen." I asked him once about that, and he fielded the question with some absurd story about having discovered long ago that once he got his hand to start making the wiggles for the two *N*s, he couldn't stop and would go on and write three *N*s. So he decided to abort the process after only one *N*. This supposed lack of manual control is a little hard to swallow coming from the man who could play an unbroken stream of thirty-second notes faster and cleaner than any other pianist on the face of the earth.

As long as I knew him, Gould maintained a residence at 110 St. Clair West in Toronto. Even now, it makes me uncomfortable to write that address because, throughout all the years of our relationship, one of the sacred vows I had to abide by was never to reveal either his home address or his home phone number to anyone. Of course, Columbia Records had both these pieces of information on file, but as each new producer or secretary was hired by the department, they too had to swear to keep this trust. Gould protected his privacy in a strange way. He claimed he was fearful about going to a public restaurant because of the possibility of being recognized and pestered by "fans." So, in a peculiar attempt to preserve his privacy, Gould would show up at a dining establishment at an unlikely hour wearing an overcoat and dark glasses in the middle of May. His convoluted efforts at anonymity made him the first person you'd spot if you walked in the door.

According to my files, my first investigatory trip to Toronto was in the autumn of 1970. I know that my last trip was almost exactly nine years later. When we were in full swing, I would fly to Canada as often as twice a month. Some simple math can show a rough estimate of how many of these trips I made during the near-decade of our recording in Canada. The minimum stay was two days, but on occasion it was stretched to three. In all these hundreds of days spent in Toronto, not once did I ever see the apartment on St. Clair West. We met in hotels, we met in restaurants, we met at the CBC, but I was never in that apartment. As in other mysteries, I came to the conclusion that this was no accident. Glenn was keeping me away for some specific reason, but I never found out why. In contrast, however, Ray Roberts was completely familiar with the apartment. I often heard Glenn and him discussing the proposed plan for "cleaning the place up." Maybe its physical disarray made Gould ashamed of it in some way, but not so ashamed as to keep everyone out. I also know that there was a housekeeper in his employ so the place couldn't have been in that bad shape.

There were two mysteries connected with that dwelling, and very likely there was a relationship between them. One concerned the time that Glenn moved out to live in a hotel. At first, he explained to me that he was having the apartment painted and couldn't stand the smell. Sounded reasonable. Then, as days turned into weeks, it became clear that he was enjoying the double convenience that the hotel room afforded him. He could order room service when he got hungry. Someone came in every day to clean up. But more than that, the particular place he chose was directly across the street from the offices of the CBC and only a few blocks from Eaton's. Also, the new address and especially the new phone number gave him a double layer of privacy protection.

As hard as he had tried to keep the phone and address associated with St. Clair West a secret, he became aware that over the years the information was somehow leaking out. He used to use the CBC as his official business location if someone wanted to contact him for an interview. But now, with the St. Clair apartment becoming less protected, he shifted everything down one level. In other words, he was a little less protective of the home phone number and would occasionally give it out to people—knowing that he was no longer living there and the caller would simply run into his answering service. The one to guard with our lives now was the number of the Four Seasons Hotel. As weeks turned into months and then to years, it was clear that he had established a new address—and an expensive one at that, considering that he maintained both places simultaneously.

The mystery of Glenn's moving out of his own apartment was made even more tantalizing by a rumor that was circulating around New York musical circles. There were people willing to swear that a woman had moved in with him at St. Clair West. Under normal circumstances, one would think that in Toronto this kind of a statement could be proved or disproved easily. However, Glenn kept such a tight control over what he would reveal—to anyone—about his personal life that it was not hard to see why no one had good information about his activities. Also, one must recognize that even if it were true, "keeping house" with a woman is no reason to move out of the selfsame dwelling! After years and years of working for Gould, Ray Roberts said: "I think I know all there is to know about Glenn Gould Limited [Glenn's corporation], but I still know nothing about Glenn Gould." Ray went on to indicate that he had come to the conclusion that a surefire way to cause an irrevocable rift in his relationship with Gould was to ask any question regarding the pianist's social relations with the opposite sex.

In many ways, Gould displayed a kind of arrested development; certainly in his emotional behavior. From a social standpoint, it seemed clear to me that Glenn viewed women with a kind of prepubescent naïveté. His fantasies at once exhibited the immaturity of a teenager and the creative sophistication that could come only with his chronological years.

In our early days together, there were two people in the employ of Columbia Records who caused his fertile imagination to weave a most remarkable scenario. James Goodfriend was, for a time, the Masterworks literary editor. This gave him the responsibility of coordinating, editing, and sometimes writing the liner notes that accompanied the records produced by the classical department. Certainly Glenn knew him, not only as a casual company acquaintance but in a more active sense. When Glenn opted to write the notes for one of his own albums—as he did on twenty-five occasions—Goodfriend was his editor.* Eventually James Goodfriend left Columbia Records to become the classical music editor of *Stereo Review* magazine.

During this same period, a young lady named Carol Hodgdon was working directly for the Masterworks Department. In the course of Gould's relationship with CBS, he visited the office many times and, during these trips, became acquainted with her. She was an intelligent, personable woman and would always stop and chat with Glenn when he came in. After a while, it seemed to us that if he didn't run into Carol accidentally, Gould would go out of his way to find her. It was thought, in archaic parlance, that Glenn was "sweet on her." Apparently her feelings about him were not amorously motivated because soon after, she married James Goodfriend.

In the years that followed, Gould was positive that he was on the wrong end of a "bad review" campaign waged by *Stereo Review*. As his closeness with *High Fidelity* magazine (*Stereo Review*'s arch rival) increased—evidenced by the number of substantial articles he wrote for them, as well as occasional feature pieces they wrote about him— he would constantly tell me that he was sure that *Stereo Review* was "out to get him." It was true that he had received a certain amount of bad press from them, but I found it hard to believe that there was a conscious program afoot to malign him. In fact, on one occasion when

---

*During his lifetime, Glenn was nominated several times for the record industry's yearly "Academy Awards"—the Grammy—but was never proclaimed the winner, except once. For the recording of the Hindemith Piano Sonatas, Glenn wrote the essay on the back of the jacket and on March 2, 1974, he was awarded the Grammy for Best Liner Notes of 1973. He did not win in the category of Best Solo Performance until the year after his death, when his new recording of the *Goldberg Variations* won both the "Performance" and "Record of the Year" awards for the year 1982.

I ran into Goodfriend at a social gathering, I asked him point-blank whether he or his magazine was harboring any ill feelings toward Gould. He denied it most emphatically and pointed to several favorable reviews that the magazine had published, which Gould perhaps had conveniently overlooked when he formulated his hypothesis.

I told Glenn of my conversation with Goodfriend, but he was not dissuaded. When I asked him why he was so sure that a personal vendetta was being waged, he confidentially told me that he thought he knew the real reason: Goodfriend was secretly jealous of him because of his friendship with Carol. Glenn fantasized that during Goodfriend's courting period, Carol was showing the pianist just a little too much attention, and Goodfriend resented Gould after that. The whole episode appeared to me like something one could unearth from a teenager's diary. Glenn must have been in his mid-thirties at the time.

Outside of his conversations with Carol Hodgdon, I saw Glenn in the company of a woman only once, and that woman was Cornelia Foss, the wife of the composer Lucas Foss. Prior to our actual meeting, I had already perceived that she and Glenn had developed a close friendship. Needless to say, it was not possible to tell whether the relationship could be categorized as "romantic." From time to time Glenn would bring her name up in conversations in a very matter-of-fact way, much the same as one would mention a marriage partner. "Well, I was not at all sure whether to believe the guy's story, but Cornelia felt he was telling the truth so . . ." I had also heard of a rather weird but touching relationship that they maintained on the telephone. There would be long, long evening calls between him in Toronto and her somewhere in New York. They would talk and talk until they fell asleep—each with the phone still at their ears. I never ceased to wonder about the size of Glenn's phone bill.

I saw them together in New York during November 1967 when Glenn had arranged with the Public Broadcasting System (PBS) a special showing of a television production he had recently completed. I recall that it centered on Mozart. One of the reasons for the occasion was that Herbert von Karajan was in town and, being a self-confessed fan of Gould and his art, he was interested in seeing the show. So the following people were gathered together in a screening room: Glenn and Cornelia, Karajan and his strikingly beautiful new wife, myself and a few assorted PBS types.

It was a different Glenn Gould that I saw during that day. Instead of the self-absorbed center of attention, I witnessed an attentive escort to Cornelia. Was she comfortable? Could he get her anything? My current mental image of them during the actual showing of the tape is of Cornelia sitting in a large lounge chair and Glenn perching on the arm of same, sort of draped over the back of it. Throughout this period, there was no doubt that Cornelia Foss held a special place in his life. I had gleaned the same message as Ray Roberts concerning the sagacity of staying clear of questions on this subject, so my information was confined to what Glenn himself chose to reveal. Because of that, it was not well defined exactly when her name began to fade from his conversations. I just sort of sat up one day and realized that he had ceased speaking of her. She was never mentioned again. In the remaining years of our association, I was never aware of another female companion, but that, of course, was no reliable indication that one did not exist. Besides that, I learned from Ray Roberts of the strong possibility that there was a social relationship between Glenn and Roxolana Roslak, the soprano who collaborated with us in the recording of Hindemith's *Das Marienleben*. In fact, during our last phone call together, I had the unmistakable impression that there was a woman with him as we spoke. It has occurred to me that the termination of our friendship might have been somehow related to my unwitting intrusion.

Over the years, I was besieged with a barrage of questions from curious gossipmongers, all wanting an answer to "the big question"—Was Gould a homosexual? By now the reader should at least be able to anticipate the beginning of my response: Gould was such a master at keeping control over exactly what he would allow one to know about his private life that I cannot make a definitive statement. I can only reply that in the fifteen years I knew him, never did I see any evidence to that effect. Of course, never did I see or hear evidence to the contrary. My own conjecture was that he was a kind of neuter. His own emotional involvement with his music—clear to see on his face as he played—was so intense that one might conclude that the piano was his mistress. I remember a conversation I had years ago with one of my colleagues. He had heard that it was a documented fact that a musician, in the midst of a performance, could become so emotionally involved that he (or she?) could actually experience a sexual climax while playing. I have no personal evidence of this fascinating theory, but the story does tend to leave the door open on the question of whether Gould actually needed female (or male) sexual companionship.

3

I once said to Glenn that he possessed the most prodigious intellect with which I had ever come into contact. I believed it then and I believe it now. Gould's brain was his chief asset, his most loyal companion, and, in the end, his mortal enemy. His ability to see the totality of a musical composition, no matter how lengthy, in one all-encompassing snapshot gave him the perspective within which to weave a carefully graded tapestry. It was almost as if time moved at a different speed for him; the rest of us hopelessly left behind, bogged down in tiny details.

I am convinced that Glenn's concept of time was more compressed than most people's. Sometimes, the longest interval would seem like an instant for him. Although this ability to see an entire musical movement in one blink had the undeniable advantage of enabling him to craft beautifully proportioned structures, it sometimes created a side problem for his listeners. Simply stated, it was this:

Glenn had little or no empathy for the effect that a presentation of extraordinary length had on his audience. Another, blunter way of putting it was that much of what he did was too long, or too slow, sometimes bordering on the tedious or boring. I'm convinced that he had no notion of how long a given span of time felt to the listener because, for him, it was subjectively much shorter. I have purposely used the words *what he did* because I observed that this effect was not just limited to musical performances. True, he was capable of executing a slow movement at a tempo that was at times exactly one-half of the speed requested by the composer; but in nonmusical endeavors he also seemed unaware of the time he was consuming. His talks were often too long; the plot of a simple humorous anecdote could wind its way through many twists and turns with subplots and diversions before reaching its punch line. Again, I'm sure this was only because he saw the entire trip in one swoop before he even commenced the journey. The rest of us were very often bored.

Glenn's intellectual interest found reward in areas other than music. He knew more about the politics of the United States than the average resident here. (Don't forget, he was a "foreigner" who was quite proud of his nationality and never once entertained the notion of becoming an American citizen.) How many Americans have an ongoing interest in Canadian current events? Geography was not exactly my strong suit, and one of the long-running gags we maintained was his "merciless" ribbing of me for not knowing exactly where Colorado was on an unmarked map. He did.

In the area of recording, he took an avid interest in the process itself and, although he was not able to explain the workings of an amplifier, he was (in the main) unique among most of his musical colleagues in his ability at least to conceptualize the steps in a technical process. Certainly, when it came to tape splicing, he undoubtedly understood it as well as a professional editor.

• • •

In the light of all the above, it was always amazing when I would stumble into one of his blind spots. The quintessential example of this happened early in our association while we were still recording in New York—more precisely, while we were *editing* in New York. I remember many evenings spent with him in the old home of the Columbia recording studios on Seventh Avenue deep in the process of choosing takes for an upcoming album. Sooner or later, either my hunger or the hunger of our staff engineer would cause us to take a dinner break. It was never *his* hunger, as Gould very often went for long stretches without eating solid food. On the day of a recording he wouldn't eat at all. He claimed fasting sharpened the mind. For me, such starvation would simply induce a headache. In the evening, one very convenient place to have a civilized meal was a restaurant quite near the studio called the Stockholm. One night, while eating a pleasant supper there, a question about editing came up. It concerned the process Glenn loved to call "regeneration." It has always been a fascinating topic for me since it has deep philosophical ramifications as well as the clear technical risks.

Briefly stated, the process concerns the wholesale "lifting" of a portion of a recorded musical performance and using it to do double duty by substituting it for another place in the music where the composer has written the same notes. One very obvious example exists in most "classical" sonatas when the score calls for the entire opening section to be repeated. Occasionally the player makes an error in the first or second performance of these pages, but not both times. When figuring out the editing plan for the area, it is often advisable to consider using a section from the "good" reading to cover the same notes in the "bad" iteration. Sometimes a whole passage may be sonically "Xeroxed" and substituted for a less-inspired rendition of the same music. Now, the controversial aspect of the practice is that some musicians feel that even

64

though the composer has asked the performer to repeat, identically, a number of measures in his composition, in fact—musicians not being automatons—there will be subtle differences in the way the reiteration will sound when compared to the first reading. The argument is that if the tape editor regenerates one of these performances and uses it both times, he will have created two playings so identical that the human variation (a "plus" in these musicians' world) will be absent and the entire effect will be inferior. Glenn, by the way, did not feel this way at all and in certain Bach dance movements would not even bother to record the "repeat." He knew from the start that he wanted the two performances to be as identical as possible, a goal perfectly achieved by regeneration.

So that the reader can understand what the nature of Gould's blind spot was, I must delve further into a technical explanation that will serve as background. I am well aware that by trying one last time to explain this process, I may wind up writing an essay that reveals my inadequacies as a teacher rather than anything to do with Glenn Gould's intellectual blind spots. In any case, I will brave it with the secret underlying hope that wherever Glenn is, he may finally comprehend the procedure.

The tapes that come directly from a recording session are very often multi-track recordings. This means that before a final master, which will spawn the finished record, can be produced, the tracks must be electronically combined, or "mixed" together, so that only two remain—the ones that will be called the left and right stereo channels. The mixing process merely involves playing the original, multi-track tape on one machine, combining the sound of the various tracks by passing them through a mixing console, and then finally recording the newly created two-track mix-down on a second recorder. The final master is always a copy of the original tapes. Although most listeners cannot detect any serious degradation to the audio signal as a result of copying it, theoretically some does indeed exist, and the producer is always a bit wary of extending the process too far; that is, of making a copy of a copy. In the industry, these various reproductions are classified by numbering their "generations." The original tape is the first generation, a copy of it is known as a second-generation tape, a copy of *it* is called the third generation, and so on.

Now, when the performance is spliced together, the original (first-generation) tapes from the recording session are actually cut. So, the spliced but not yet mixed multi-track master is still a first-generation tape, as it is constituted from pieces of first-generation tapes physically attached to each other. Next, in the mixing stage, the second-generation final master is produced. Here is where the process gets tricky.

When the first-generation spliced master is constructed, the editing engineer has nothing in his hands at the predetermined point where the "clone" is to be introduced. Because the performer played the spot only *once* correctly, there is only *one* bit of tape with those measures properly executed. However, to make our scheme work, we need to have *two* copies of the "good" material. For the spliced multi-track tape to contain a complete performance (including the regeneration), the engineer would have to make a multi-track copy of the "perfect" bars and splice that back into the first-generation master at the place where the imperfect performance actually took place. Now a master has been created that is "first generation" for 99 percent of the time, but has an inserted little piece of "second-generation" tape polluting its purity.

As we follow the situation through the mixing process—where, of necessity, one generation gets added to everything—we wind up with a tape that is "second generation" 99 percent of the time with a little bit of "third-generation" material included. But this needn't occur. If we resist the temptation to make the first-generation tape complete and musically correct (and be satisfied with a bit of blank tape inserted at the "imperfect" point) and postpone the regeneration process until the mixing is being performed, we have created an advantageous situation. The fact is that the whole final mixed tape is a copy to begin with, so during mixing, we can spin off as many duplicates of the crucial "perfect" passage as we like; they all will be "second generation." Now it is an easy matter to splice one of these clones into the blank spot in the mixed master and complete the performance—without having to resort to using "third-generation" material. That's the process. Ironically, with the modern-day introduction of digital recording, every generation of tape is as perfect as the first, which makes the producer's reservation about unnecessary cloning become an obsolete concern. However, at the time of this story, even the Dolby system had not yet been invented, so the fear of copying was real.

So, to get back to the tale, the first time I ever played for Glenn a spliced first-generation tape of a performance that included the necessity of regeneration, he was surprised to encounter that little bit of blank tape inserted in the middle. I tried to explain the reasoning set forth above but he didn't grasp it. Now, here we were in the Stockholm Restaurant in a nice relaxed atmosphere and the question came up again. Well, after having experienced the wonder of his feats of memorization, I could not accept the possibility that Gould could not comprehend what was, to me, a rather simple concept. Therefore, I was determined to explain, once and for all, why I didn't choose to create the clone at that early stage and why it was better if I waited till the mixing process. As I began speaking, I saw a thin haze settle over his face, and the more I talked the more I saw that giant intellect shut down. He simply would not absorb it—a clear example of a true mental block. In years to come, he would refer to the experience of that evening whenever he sensed another block forming—on any subject—by saying: "Sir, I think this is turning into one of those 'Stockholm conversations.'" This was my cue to lay out and give it up as a bad job.

• • •

If his capacity to absorb the niceties of certain technical operations was limited in some way, Gould's brain offered some interesting compensatory features. He possessed a rare psychoacoustical ability known as *absolute pitch*—sometimes called perfect pitch. It is possible for someone possessing this gift permanently to "remember" the pitch of every note. If one wakes such an individual from a sound sleep and says: "Sing G-flat," the response will be accurate. Alternatively, if a gifted Robinson Crusoe were rescued from his island and the first sound he heard was the ship's bell on the vessel that would carry him to civilization, he would be able to say with confidence: "The pitch of that bell is D-sharp."

As one who has spent a lifetime being astounded by this phenomenon, I have always found it ironic that so many pianists are blessed with it. The irony stems from the fact that the pitch of the string that will sound when the pianist plays a particular note has been carefully preset by the tuner, and the accuracy of the player's ability to predict what it will sound like before it is struck is a practically useless talent. On the other hand, it always seems unfair that someone like a timpani player, who has to tune his drums to specific pitches in the middle of a performance while the orchestra is intoning a passage with no close relationship to the notes he is seeking, is most often denied this most desirable ability to "pick the notes out of the air."

The majority of us, who do not have perfect pitch, must rely on a variety of tricks and learned techniques to establish the sound of a given note, while our gifted colleagues sail through the problem as if it were the most natural thing in the world. To summarize the relationship between a musician so blessed and the more "normal" kind, I can do no better than to quote two sentences that were part of a conversation I had with the first individual I had ever met who possessed this talent. At the height of my amazement, I said: "But how do you *know*

that's E-flat?" He simply pointed to the wall and responded: "How do *you* know that's green?"

Notwithstanding the fact that timpanists think that
heaven played a cruel joke in the distribution of this gift,
even pianists find homey little tasks to perform with their
extra capability, and these activities do indeed make life
in the world of music easier for them. I know that to Gould
the natural divisions of a composition were distinguished
by their keys. It was very common during a recording
session for him to say to me: "Let me start over again
from the F-sharp minor section." I then had to flip through
the score at a rather fast clip—analyzing key centers as I
went—in order to locate the spot he had in mind. You
see, for him the section in F-sharp minor was as instantly
recognizable and as obviously unique as an allegro suddenly coming to life in the midst of an andante; it had a
sound of its own. For me, I had no idea that my experience in listening to the piece had taken me through the
key of F-sharp minor. I simply had to analyze everything
I saw on the page and find the section by its "finger-
prints," so to speak.

To illustrate the extent to which Glenn depended on
this gift, I must relate a story he told me. One day, while
driving in his car, he turned on the radio and was greeted
by a musical performance already in progress. As he drove,
he became aware that the piece sounded familiar to him,
but he could not place it. The more he listened, the more
he was sure that he knew it, but also the more frustrated
he became by its elusiveness. In fact, the performance came
to an end with Gould still trying in vain to place it. When
the radio announcer identified the title and composer,
Glenn realized what had happened. He had known the
composition for years, but this radio performance was some
sort of arrangement of the original, and it was played in
a different key. So closely was the tonality of the traditional performance linked to the essence of the composition (in Gould's mind) that the transposition to another

69

key made this new rendition sound completely different to him. Interestingly, the entire experience would have offered no problem and would have had no impact for the majority of "average" musicians who would have correctly identified the piece in the first place—being blithely unaware that it was sounding in the wrong key.

Once Glenn said that if the gift of absolute pitch were suddenly taken away from him, he was sure he wouldn't be able to function in music. I made some joke about how he had simply gotten "soft" and then seriously asked him to imagine what it was like for the rest of us who knew no other reality but this kind of "color blindness" to pitch. We spent considerable time over the years, batting about this question.

One day, in the midst of a long talk, Glenn suddenly interrupted the conversation, wheeled around, pointed to me, and quickly said: "Sing the opening of Beethoven's Fifth!" Well, I did, but it was not in the right key. Glenn had reasoned that I had heard this piece so many times in my life that, by sheer instinct, I might just be able to reproduce it in the key Beethoven chose. No such luck. Not dissuaded, Gould tried to surprise me at other odd moments with other requests in order to see if I could ever comply correctly. I always failed the test—as we both would have predicted. Many times he would repeat his demand for Beethoven's Fifth, just to see if I was consistent. I was not. The darned thing would come out in whatever key it chose—hardly ever C minor.

Then, one fateful day, he asked me to sing "The Star-Spangled Banner." After I did, he said: "Hm . . . that was B-flat; probably the key in which you've heard it most frequently—military bands and the like." I smiled and the incident passed. But months later, once again he surprised me with the same request. It is important to understand that the element of surprise is vital to the playing of this game. In fact, if I took too long to think, I would voluntarily disqualify myself from that round. The object, which we both recognized, was to try to elicit a

70

natural, spontaneous response to see if my supposed lack of this ability was simply a matter of musical inhibition. So once again I sang the opening of "The Star-Spangled Banner." Instantly and triumphantly, Gould proclaimed it to be in B-flat. My interest increased.

Over the course of maybe ten years, we played this game repeatedly, and if his request truly came "from out of the blue"—with no undue influence upon me from having just come from listening to some other music—my performance of "The Star-Spangled Banner" was always in the key of B-flat, while my attempts at other well-known compositions would wander all over the tonal map. The trouble was that it was not possible to draw any real scientific conclusion from this protracted series of experiments—except, I dread to contemplate, that perhaps my interest in U.S. politics was a lot deeper than I suspected.

But other games were everywhere and, as long as he could win them, Gould enjoyed playing. The connecting thread that tied all such endeavors together was the triumph of intellect as the winning strategy. At great length, Glenn would condemn the concept of competitive sports. He loudly proclaimed that it was wrong for two people (or groups of people) to pit their strength or skill against each other for the purpose of *winning*. If one wishes to be uncharitable, it is easy to state that having shown absolutely no predilection toward any athletic sport, Glenn was really speaking out against any contest that *he* could not win.

But there were a lot of contests he could win. It does not seem to me to be stretching a point to say that the whole arena of musical performance was a kind of contest. Simply ask any young instrumentalist who has just devoted fifteen years to intense study and practice and has achieved an admirably high level of performance and who cannot get a job because there are only a limited number of positions open in the restrictive world of concert promotion. Gould possessed a technique that put him in a class by himself. His musical knowledge and instincts were to be marveled at. If he hadn't espoused the eccentric course of being reclusive, shunning concerts and flaunting highly individualistic readings of the standard repertoire, it is likely that he would have risen far above the position he attained in general popularity. As it was, he was a phenomenon in that he was able to disprove the popularly held theory that without continual concert activity, significant record sales were impossible. For eighteen and one-half years he maintained a respectable recording career without the benefit of a single public appearance. If that's not called "winning," I don't know what is. To release the umpteenth recording of a Beethoven sonata in a glutted marketplace and strive for notice and record sales is, by anyone's definition, entering a contest—with the goal of winning.

Once in the late 1960s he and I were talking about war and the frightening prospect of joining the armed forces. Putting on the clean white robes of the pacifist, he told me that it would be unthinkable for him to imagine himself entering battle and holding a weapon to be used against his fellow man. With a faraway look in his eye, he stared up into the corner of the room and said that he could, however, envision himself secreted deep within an underground bunker, surrounded by electronic paraphernalia and acting as the mastermind in planning the (winning) strategy to conquer the enemy.

On a less frightening plane, he dearly loved guessing games. This passion would very often take the form of a customized version of Twenty Questions. The modification was simple: Don't count! I can't recall when this pastime got started for it seems as if it were always there. Excuses for playing were everywhere. In the normal flow of conversation, instead of merely imparting a piece of information, one would issue the challenge: "I've got something for you to guess!" Of course, there was the tacit assumption that the "punch line" was indeed something of sufficient interest to warrant invoking the game.

From my point of view, subjects like: "Joe Smith got fired or promoted"; "Your recording has just won a prize"; "I've just left the employ of CBS," and so on, all would qualify as good topics for Twenty Questions. From his perspective, juicy subjects worth spending fifteen or twenty minutes of international telephone charges would be "I've just signed a deal to do the music for *Slaughterhouse Five*," or "You'll never guess who telephoned me today!"

With a kind of childlike enthusiasm, one could literally "hear" his face light up if the magic words were spoken: "I've got something for you to guess!" He would virtually rub his hands together in glee and then begin: "Is it a person located within fifty miles of the New York area? . . ." Playing either side of the game would give him equal pleasure. If he was the guessor, he would set about his task with methodical preciseness. I never knew him to lose, or give up. If he was the guessee, he would settle into the calm, slightly smug, role of the Keeper of All Knowledge. Even in this capacity, he so enjoyed the game that if I was taking a long time to ferret out his secret, he would not lose patience and he would stick with it until I unearthed the information. I almost wrote: ". . . until I won," but that would never do since, as we know he would not participate in a contest that ended with one entrant being proclaimed the winner.

One of the most bizarre experiences I ever had playing this game came about from a subject I had challenged him with; having just discovered that his new recording of Scriabin and Prokofiev sonatas had gotten a favorable review in a very unlikely place—*Cosmopolitan* magazine—I told him I would read him the paragraph and then he had to guess the source. Virtually as I opened my mouth, he interrupted to caution me: "You remember my policy: I only hear favorable reviews these days." The implication here is that there were *other* days, days gone by, when his policy would not prohibit him from hearing a bad review. Well, I think that this was so, but I was never aware of the "transition." Like so many aspects of Gould's life, one day you looked around and a whole new regime was in full force.

After assuring him that it was indeed favorable, I read it. He started guessing right away, sensing that the publication must be unusual or I would not have thought that the whole exercise was worthy of a Twenty Questions approach. He made several guesses and almost ran out of American magazines but, with a little nudge from me, he got it. I mentioned that I had thought he would find it amusing ever since my wife had brought it to my attention.

Then it started: "What's Gen doing reading *Cosmopolitan?* Well, you may tell her for me that I disapprove, I strongly disapprove. . . . I think that Gen should end her subscription immediately." I interjected that she was not a subscriber but just picked it up once in a while. He went on: "Then she must resist—completely—that's the end of that." I tried to change the subject, mentioning something about another recording we had been discussing. However, when the steam from my effort slackened off, he returned immediately to his original attack. "I'm very disturbed with Gen. I really think that's got to stop."

If this had been a conversation with anyone else (but then, how *could* it have been a conversation with anyone else?), I probably would have said something that could not be reproduced here; perhaps the punch line to the joke that describes a job that combines sex and travel. But with Glenn, I had to take a deep breath and gently suggest that Genevieve was a mature, intelligent adult and was free to select her own reading material. He was not dissuaded. "You could go around tearing out certain pages . . . very effective if she sort of got up in the morning and found that the page she wanted to look at again wasn't there." The reader must understand and believe that Gould was totally serious and quite a bit exercised on the subject. I never did find out what there was about *Cosmopolitan,* or the head of the publication, Helen Gurley

74

Brown, that elicited from him such a strong reaction, but I was somehow able to defuse the conversation and change the topic. The next morning, when I related the story to Gen, she too demonstrated that she had long lived in a home shadowed by the presence of Glenn Gould; she simply smiled.

Twenty Questions was not the only game he relished. We had a telephone conversation in late 1971 that was devoted almost exclusively to a little book he had just bought for $1.95. The book described, in great detail, a test that had been devised by some German (I think) psychologist that purported to use the subject's preferences for various colors as the index of his personality. The little volume even had eight cutout cards that were to be displayed before the volunteer, each one containing a sample of a scientifically chosen color. The choices were red, yellow, blue, violet, green, brown, black, and gray.

Glenn had studied the book, taken the test himself, become very perturbed with the analysis that the text made of his choices, and now was calling me (at international telephone rates) to spend something in excess of one hour describing the test and then administering it to me. Someone might wonder how or why I put myself through these marathon phone calls—especially when they had no direct connection with work. I think there were two reasons. First, see: "The Artist—How to Keep Him Happy"; and second, I had developed a morbid curiosity concerning exactly how long he would keep spending money on these frivolous calls.

After taking the test—that, I must say (amazing though it is), seemed to come close to describing the personality traits I thought I possessed—Glenn went on to describe in detail his own experience with this new toy. He was very much upset about some of the inaccuracies the analysis foisted on him, but the one thing that really bothered him was the statement that someone with his particular combination of color preferences was a person living under great daily stress and, furthermore, there was the likelihood that this person might develop coronary problems. Well, that did it! He felt it was completely irresponsible for a book distributed to the public to offhandedly make that kind of alarmist statement. Of course, the fact that in a short time Gould developed high blood pressure and then succumbed to a stroke a few years later serves to add a spine-chilling irony to the whole experience.

Glenn's reactions to colors had always been a little abnormal. After I took the test, our conversation continued with his saying: "The only colors I can tolerate are blue and gray. . . . I never wear anything else but blue and gray. Every wall I ever had painted is painted gray. I cannot bear bright colors."

While on the subject of his clothes, it is significant to point out that his socks never matched. Usually one was dark blue and the other one gray or black. I stress the word *never* because I have always suspected that this color scheme was not accidental. If one fantasizes a stereotypical image of the "artist" whose concentration centers only on ethereal matters and certainly not on the mundane questions of daily attire, one can easily visualize a bureau drawer filled with blue and black socks without any pattern of pairing. Every morning, the distracted man sticks his hand in the drawer, randomly withdraws two socks, and puts them on without bothering to notice if they match. Now, the laws of chance teach us that the odds of selecting a matching pair are fifty–fifty. So, if Glenn was simply not interested in wearing uniformly colored socks and made his choice randomly, it is reasonable to assume that at least some of the time (if not exactly half of the time) he would have blundered into two of a kind. The fact that they never matched seems to me (and the dictates of probability) to indicate the presence of control, just as much as if he had wanted them to match.

When Glenn was four or five years old, some woman gave him a present of a red toy fire engine. Despite the issue that no other color would have been appropriate for such a vehicle, the fact that it was red caused him to fly into a tantrum. He recalled that he became completely uncontrollable and had to be calmed down at some length. Exactly what there was about the color red was never made completely clear, but he stated that "I wouldn't have, as a child, any toy that was colored red at all." He went on: "I hate clear days; I hate the sunlight; I hate yellow. . . . To long for a gray day was, for me, the ultimate that one could achieve in the world."

Whether bright days were repugnant to him because they tended to display the colors he despised, or whether red and yellow were unfortunate reminders of "bad" weather conditions, always remained a mystery to me. However, his strong feelings along these lines were undeniable. I know, for example, that one of his favorite album covers was the one wrapping his recording of the three popular Beethoven piano sonatas (*Moonlight, Pathetique, Appassionata*) and this displayed a picture of him in very bleak, snowy surroundings. It was not just that he liked the photograph, but rather what it represented. "It's very *me*," he said.

Whether natural or self-induced, there was no question that his demeanor and (more important) his productivity at recording sessions were very often pegged to the weather. He made it a point to show me that he would sail through the most difficult of compositions with great spirit and determination if it was gray and/or raining outside.

Weather permitting, life with Glenn Gould could occasionally provide some of the most bizarre experiences imaginable. While his true involvement with women will always be a mystery, there was another facet to "the opposite sex" that was more like a comedy—although sometimes a black one. The kind of public image that Gould projected—intelligent, artistic, eccentric, reclusive, handsome, famous, *single*—apparently was irresistibly appealing to a certain type of woman, and from time to time Glenn would receive fan mail of a rather suggestive type.

Sometimes I would learn about it, but more often than not, he wouldn't even bother to mention it, probably because he had gotten so used to it.

On occasion, like a genetic mutant that has fortuitously found a way to exist in a hostile environment, one of these women would exhibit a level of ingenuity and/or perseverance that would enable her to slip through a few layers of Gould's security system. I don't know that any of them ever made it in to the central core, thereby achieving an actual face-to-face encounter with Gould himself, but some came awfully close.

Back in the late 1960s, there was the case of one Elisheva Kaufman. This enterprising young woman had been in concentrated pursuit of Gould, having signaled her intent with a letter asking for a meeting. The intervening years have sanded away some of the details, but I think she started off utilizing the ploy that she was a music student, or a writer, or some other plausible self-description that could be used as an entrée to meet Glenn. Because Gould's Toronto address was such a well-kept secret, a lot of mail came to him in care of Columbia Records. When such a letter arrived, the people in the mail room automatically forwarded it to the Masterworks Department from where the letter eventually was routed to my desk. Nearly always, I sent it up to Toronto; on occasion, if a trip was imminent, I would deliver it by hand. Very rarely, if I mentioned that I possessed such a missive while speaking to Glenn by phone, he might instruct me to dispose of it.

Right in the middle of the Elisheva Kaufman incident, Glenn came down to New York for recording. In fact, at the moment in question, he was in my office at the CBS Building (wryly dubbed "Black Rock") discussing our schedule. Suddenly the phone rang and I was informed that Goddard Lieberson's secretary was on the line. Lieberson was the president of Columbia Records. *All* of it. His position, when seen through the eyes of a mere producer in the Masterworks Department, seemed about as remote as the president of the United States' being viewed by the mayor of some little town in Colorado. Just imagine what this hypothetical mayor would say if he were told that the White House was on the line. Ditto for me. I answered the call and was asked if Glenn Gould were there. Glenn, of course, knew Goddard personally so there was absolutely no reason to maintain our security.

Therefore, guns lowered, I answered in the affirmative. The secretary then went on to say that a young lady had come to her desk and was asking for Glenn Gould . . . name of Elisheva. I didn't give her the time to finish the sentence. Luckily (for me, not for Glenn), Lieberson's office was right down the hall from my own, and I bolted out the door and ran for it. In the meantime Gould, who by now had gathered what had happened on the phone, was barricading himself within my office. Six seconds later I was with Lieberson's secretary and she told me that Miss Kaufman had suddenly turned and run off into the foyer, thence to disappear within a stairwell.

A bit disappointed at having missed the quarry, I returned to my office, gave the agreed-upon identification signal, used my key to open the lock, and found Glenn cowering in a crouched position behind the door. Apparently, during the time I was out in the hall, his active imagination had conjured up a scenario where Elisheva, pearl-handled revolver drawn, was stalking the corridors of Black Rock in order to rid the world of a certain Canadian pianist.

It was in the ensuing postchase debriefing that the "Kazdin Detective Agency" was born. I promised Glenn that I would do whatever I could to find out who this woman was and to try to get her to stop pursuing him. Either from a return address on her letter or a phone number she had left with Lieberson's secretary, I was able to begin my investigation. I was amazed at her luck, which caused her to appear at the very moment Glenn was within one hundred feet. There was almost no way she could have known he was in town or in Black Rock. I marveled at her ingenuity at having figured out that by going through Lieberson's office (even though no one there could have been of any practical use to her), she would be able to equip herself with a powerful tool with which to find out where Gould was. I set myself to the task of tracking down this mystery woman. I found out rather quickly that the phone number I was given was her work number. Luckily, the man who answered my call found my story credible enough to stay on the phone while we put the pieces together.

First, I learned there was no person working there named Elisheva Kaufman, but somehow we were able to deduce who the likely party was. Furthermore, the man admitted that the suspected young woman had previously demonstrated her proclivities for the unconventional and he had long since harbored suspicions that something was not quite right with her. After giving him my assurance that we were not going to do her bodily harm, or press any kind of legal charges, he gave me her real name and address.

Exactly how our eventual phone conversation materialized, I no longer remember, but I believe that she called me—still pretending to be Elisheva Kaufman. I calmly confronted her with what we had discovered. "Look," I said, "you're not a student musician (or whatever it was that she was masquerading as), you're not Elisheva Kaufman, you're Carol —— and you live at thus-and-so address. Now, why don't you leave us alone?" At this point she dropped the act and told me that all she ever wanted to do was talk to Glenn Gould. I explained to her the extent of the panic she had caused and went on to say that whatever chance of contact she might have had if she had pursued the whole affair with some decorum was now hopelessly lost. I assured her that Glenn was now scared of her and would never meet with her. I think she got the idea, because she apologized and we never heard from her again. The name of Elisheva Kaufman persisted in our conversations for years and was utilized by Glenn as a kind of calibration mark against which to measure the intrusions of other young women in future encounters. Also, the Kazdin Detective Agency lived on to provide Glenn with occasional bits of information not readily available to him.

Another, much sadder, situation existed for many years. The accurate details of *this* case are readily available to me, but a sense of compassion prevents me from including any specific bits of information that might identify the person involved. This exposure could serve only to inflict emotional pain and provide no other advantage. I will resort to pseudonyms in place of the individual's name and city of residence.

Among the various letters that were received in my office to be forwarded to Gould, there would often be included an envelope from Portland, Oregon. The handwriting was always the same, and it became clear that these letters formed a continuing chain. One day Glenn told me a little about the author. Her name was Alice Barker, and he had been receiving these missives for some time. He confided in me that it was a matter of some concern to him since he perceived Alice as "a dear woman" whom he had no desire to wound in any way. However, he was being bothered by the receipt of these letters—which he had never answered or acknowledged. He didn't want to write to her to tell her to desist for fear of hurting her and perhaps setting off a more serious reaction. On the other hand, he really did not wish to deal with the situation, or in any way be reminded of its existence.

I suggested the following solution, which he readily accepted. Since all the letters from Portland were easy to identify, by me as well as any secretary in the Masterworks Department, I would merely request that any time such an envelope arrived, it should be delivered directly to me for special handling. On no account would it be forwarded to Gould. Glenn had instructed me simply to destroy the letters, but naturally I revealed this mandate

81

to no one. The complicated part of the story is that Glenn never knew that I carried these missives home where I opened and read them. Some kind of compulsive, retentive urge caused me to save them. The collection consists of 174 letters covering the period from October 20, 1974, to February 23, 1978. By keeping them, I reasoned that I would have in no way violated Glenn's twin goals: not to upset Alice and not to upset Glenn. Neither one of them ever knew of my intervention and only now, if she is still alive and reads this, will she possibly suspect that this story concerns her.

The average letter is over twenty pages long and the frequency of composition ranges from a few hours to several weeks. By pure mathematics, they average out to arrive every seven days, but I know that some long hiatuses make this number appear higher than it really is. In full swing, Alice sent two or three a week.

They were a clear mixture of love letters (including salutations of the most endearing kind) and a simple diary, telling the daily events in the life of this sad middle-aged woman. We follow her through her troubles at work, including a change of jobs; we learn about her mother with whom she lives and seems to tolerate in a kind of love-hate relationship; we learn about her visits for psychiatric counseling; we are touched by the outpourings of love for Gould, whom she is sure will come for her some day to marry her; we discover her attachment to music; but then we learn that she is convinced that the one local radio station in Portland that plays classical music is the conduit through which Glenn has been responding to her all these years. "You knew I wanted to hear your Mozart sonatas last night!"

Between February 1978 and December 1979 (the date of my leaving CBS) there were no letters; at least I received no more. This could be due simply to some change in personnel along the chain of people that knew to forward the notes to me, or maybe she actually stopped writing. Almost five years elapsed between the last letter in the collection and Gould's death so I have no notion what took place in Portland during that period. But very soon after I was informed of Glenn's passing, my thoughts went to Alice and I wondered, if she was alive, what effect the news would have on her. If she reads this, she should take some comfort in the knowledge that Glenn did know about her and cared enough for her well-being that he did not want to injure her in any way.

4

If I were a bona fide amateur psychologist, I would be able to concoct some very nice theories about "control." Maybe I'd try to show a deep connection between the desire to control others and the ability to control one's self. Of course, I can't do that, but I can point to Gould with the knowledge that in him seethed the desire to accomplish both goals. Just once he talked about a traumatic incident that happened in his childhood. Apparently he had committed some infraction of the family rules and was engaged in an argument with his mother. He revealed to me that at the height of his rage, he felt that he was capable of inflicting serious bodily harm on this woman—perhaps even committing murder. It was only a fleeting spark of emotion, but the realization that he had, even for a split second, entertained the notion frightened him profoundly. He had suddenly come face to face with something within him that he didn't know was there.

The experience caused him to retreat into serious introspection, and when he emerged, he swore to himself that he would never let that inner rage reveal itself again. He was determined that he would live his life practicing self-control. Glenn concluded by saying that he had been successful in this endeavor and that he had never lost his temper since that first day so many years ago.

But where does control stop? Is it merely evidence of a kind of compulsion that he hardly ever submitted himself to a free-wheeling interview where the direction and results of the questioning were out of his hands? On a radio show that he hosted for some time in Toronto, he was joined by a CBC staff announcer named Ken Haslam. To the outside world, it sounded as if the two of them were actually engaging in stimulating conversation about the music featured in the show. But the truth was that every word that came out of Haslam's mouth was scripted by Gould—not to mention Glenn's responses. Ken was a real professional and therefore could read these questions in a very convincing manner, as if they were spontaneously his own. Glenn, at the same time, had also developed quite a skill at sounding surprised by an interrogation that he had himself invented. They made quite a team.

It developed to the point where transcripts of these "conversations" were printed for posterity. One rather lengthy discussion about Gould's piano transcriptions of Wagner appeared as the liner notes (actually a printed insert; it was too long to fit on the back of the record jacket) for Glenn's recording of them. It was set up to look exactly like a faithful log of a live conversation. Part of it read:

> GG . . . For instance, there's one ten-bar sequence which occurs about one and one-half minutes into the "Idyll" and in which the orchestral textures are singularly uneventful—
>
> KH Which makes for problems!

GG Which makes for problems, precisely, because, as
   I've said, a string choir can sustain one chord for
   four bars say, but a piano simply cannot—at least,
   not without making it sound like a transcription.
KH And that you were determined to avoid!
GG Indeed. You know, my first draft . . .

What a rapport those two guys had!

An even more favorite trick of Glenn's was interviewing himself. Sometimes he would actually acknowledge that it was his alter ego, but on other occasions he would stage for the microphones elaborate round-table discussions where he played all the parts. These invented characters ranged from stuffy British musicologists to New York cabdriver types to German musician/scientists (trying to calibrate the length of breathing pauses). An album released near the end of his lifetime went one step further to vitalize these fantasies. One of these multi-voiced discussions was included on the record—and so were photographs of all the participants (each bearing a remarkable family resemblance to the others). Gould was convinced that he was brilliant in these voice characterizations, but to my ears they sounded sophomoric in their stereotypical simplicity. Naturally, I was not suicidal enough to answer the question: "Isn't that terrific?" with anything other than the affirmative. Torontonians seemed to have eaten all this stuff up, and the fallout from at least three such conferences even reached CBS.

Once, when Masterworks wanted to devote one whole month's releases to the music of Bach, Glenn's newest volume of *The Well-tempered Clavier* acted as his contribution. As a promotional tool, Columbia wanted to round up a series of interviews with the artists who performed in this group of recordings and package them as a one-hour radio show to be offered to classical music stations. Glenn, of course, was approached about the convenient scheduling of such an interview. Quick as a flash, he talked the marketing staff at Masterworks out of a formal interview and had them agree to substitute a tape that he would completely produce in Toronto (at his own time and expense). What came down to us was a technical tour de force—another round-table discussion—in stereo—with overlapping conversations. Of course, the price we had to pay for this tape was that this lavish production was approximately twice as long as what we had asked him for and, naturally, could not be cut. It more or less dominated the entire radio promotion.

Probably the ultimate in media control came about when an author named Geoffrey Payzant set about the job of writing a biography of Gould, which was published in 1978 (*Glenn Gould: Music & Mind* [Toronto: Van Nostrand Reinhold Ltd., 1978]). Somehow Payzant wrote the book without extensive interviews with Gould (or any of his intimates, such as they were) and based his point of view solely on Glenn's writings, recordings, and other personal creations. It was perfect for Gould. All the fruits of a lifetime of media control came home to flower at once. All that Payzant could find in print were outpourings that Gould had meticulously controlled in the first place. So, with the pleasure of a movie director inspecting his "rushes," Gould stood by the sidelines and watched himself write this biography—with a little legwork from Payzant. Glenn said afterward that he liked the book. That was very modest of him.

A little earlier I referred to Gould's aversion to uncontrolled interviews as possibly nothing more than evidence of a compulsive personality. In truth, I don't really believe that, as I am convinced that every major component of his daily existence fell under this same stringent control. This, I feel, goes a bit beyond what one might characterize as "quirky" behavior. Without going into the very extensive and complicated rationale that accompanied his decision to stop giving concerts in 1964, the surface effect is perfect for supporting my point. Spontaneity, the *risk* of a mishap, is the very essence of a live concert; the very factor that forms the backbone of the argument that something is lost in studio recordings. A mishap? Can't have that!

To me, a record producer, the most attractive element in studio work is the fact that all components of the taped performance can be separated, individually perfected, and then re-assembled into a highly polished finished product. Gould's shunning of live performances in favor of this kind of clinical condition is a major victory for "control."

And let us not forget the carefully laundered "public information service" that Gould maintained. Everything that went out for public consumption was controlled. Probably one of the reasons that he engineered keeping me out of his media appearances was his concern that I might say or do something that would rend his carefully constructed bubble of secrecy. He had no grounds for this fear because I recognized from the start how important his persona was to maintain. If he'd have thought about it, he would have realized that if I had chosen to act indiscreetly, I had plenty of opportunities in my position at CBS. Of course, nothing like that ever happened, but yet I deem it quite possible that he was not totally convinced—or, at least, that he was unwilling to take the risk.

The desire to control his working colleagues grew from within Gould in such a natural way as to be almost unrealized by him. I believe that he never saw the truly ugly side of the story concerning my wife and *Cosmopolitan* magazine. Nor do I feel that he perceived the following incident as "going too far"—which it most certainly was.

The time was rather early in our association—perhaps 1968 or 1969. My family and I were living in an apartment complex just outside Manhattan, and, as it happened, Glenn was in New York. The opportunity never presented itself again, but on this night he was free of commitments so we invited him to visit us for dinner. At one point during the evening, we were sitting on the couch chatting when he noticed my date book lying on an end table. Here I must say something about the importance of this little book to my life in the record business. When one works in a profession that is so tied to the calendar and the clock, it is vital that an up-to-date listing of commitments be available at all times. It simply cannot be memorized reliably. Not only does this little volume contain all the important dates, places, and phone numbers necessary to conduct business, but I also use it to inscribe personal reminders and my daily expenses. I consider it a kind of private diary.

At one point in the evening, Glenn picked up my book and started to leaf through it, reading out loud various phrases that caught his eye. "Hm . . . dentist appointment next Tuesday . . . isn't $25.75 rather a lot to pay for dinner? . . . oh, happy anniversary! . . ." and so on. I felt very much trapped by this tasteless intrusion. On the one hand, my natural instinct was to snap the book from his hand and reprimand him for snooping. At the same time, I realized that the more insistent I was in demanding the book's return, the more I was acknowledging that there were contained therein some embarrassing skeletons. So I took a deep breath and let Glenn's curiosity run its course. Eventually it did, and he tossed the book back to the table. The core of the story is contained in his next words: "Well, sir, you passed!"

I wondered *what* I passed. Was it that he could find no incriminating evidence of my misconduct lurking within the pages of that volume (Personal reminder: Pick up copy of *Cosmopolitan* for Gen), or was it that I showed the strength of will (or should I say "self-control"?) to sit calmly by while he violated my privacy: "Look! I have this dog so well trained that I can hold this morsel of food right under his nose and he won't snap at it till I tell him he can have it!"

The reader must also understand that one of the most important aspects of the relationship between a record producer and his artist is a complete lack of friction. That is not to say that differences of opinion do not crop up from time to time, but major areas of controversy cannot be allowed to exist. An underlying tension would be most destructive. Therefore, I have found that I must very often lean over backward to accommodate an artist.

Just imagine the following scenario: It's near the end of a recording session. A 106-piece orchestra is collecting an aggregate union scale payment in excess of $3.50 per second. The producer says that after one little section of the Scherzo movement is remade, the recording will be complete. The conductor says that he wants to do the whole movement again. The producer reminds him that to do so would push the session over into an overtime period, which will cost in excess of $5,000. The conductor replies that if he is not allowed to do the movement again, he will walk from the podium at once and not complete the recording. What decision is applicable here? Does the producer jeopardize the tens of thousands of dollars already invested in the session just to win a point? Of course he doesn't. He takes the overtime on the chin and finishes the recording. The motto inscribed on a big plaque over the desk of every record producer is "BRING 'EM BACK ALIVE." The record must come first.

Yet we must not overlook the personality trait within the conductor that recognized he had the producer over the proverbial "barrel" and caused the man to press his advantage. The scene just described is not a fantasy, and, sadly, it is possible to retell stories of much greater abuses that egomaniacal conductors have wreaked upon their producers. Please do not misunderstand. My own code of ethical behavior dictates that if I am subject to just one such instance of unbridled egotism, I will refuse to work with the artist again. Record producers are not born masochists. But in the meantime, two effects have taken place. First, the artist has gotten one punch in. Believe me, if each musician that a producer works with cares to take his one shot, the total effect on the producer will be devastating. The second effect is, in a way, worse. With threats of walking off, suing the record company, and all other manner of retribution that the artist might possibly entertain, the producer can be in a very precarious position.* In contrast to this sea of real or imagined dangers, the prospect of Glenn Gould's probing into a private diary sounds quite tame. And *this* is the problem. This is the reason I didn't show anger. This is the cause of my personal restraint, which, I am willing to predict, most reasonable readers would find unrealistically stoic.

None of this is meant to imply that Gould had ever acted as atrociously as the conductor I described. No, he was never irrational. But in his world and in my world, having a little sport with his producer's privacy is a very easy trade for the full wrath of a capricious musical artist.

Perhaps the most complex aspect of Glenn Gould to comprehend was his feelings about morality and his fellow man. It is conceivable that all of this was a giant overreaction to the childhood incident already mentioned concerning anger toward his mother. It is vital to understand that there was quite a schism between what he said he believed in and the behavior that he actually displayed. This duality was further confused by his frequent admissions that he would *like* to practice what he preached, but, in fact, he could not.

Any conversation that we had on the subject would surely include his very strong "Christ-like" views on dealing with his brethren. Once, in a phone call following one of my early Toronto trips, we were rehashing a very disturbing (for me) incident that had just occurred. I had arrived at Eaton's anticipating a recording session, but

*By now the reader should be wondering exactly what their favorite musical personalities are really like. Lest it appear that all artists are wound up like coiled springs ready to explode in the direction of their record company, I must state that this is, of course, not the norm. Sadly, however, it *is* true in some cases. I have always wondered why these musicians seem to be hell-bent on biting the corporate hand that feeds them.

discovered that one of the little custom-built devices that was going to be put into service for the first time that evening had been wired incorrectly by the technician Glenn had hired to construct it. It wasn't a flaw that could be called a mistake—it was far too widespread for that. Either it represented ignorance of the most basic of electrical principles, or it was evidence of some twisted desire to sabotage our operation. Well, I got the fellow on the phone and let him know what I thought of his efforts. This motivated him to hustle down to the auditorium and rewire the device on the spot. My anger at the ensuing delay was quite visible, and Glenn disapproved of that.

So, here we were on the phone, having a kind of calm postmortem of the incident. Glenn was trying to convince me that verbally lashing out, as I had done, was not the appropriate reaction. Rather, he said, I should have restrained my emotions and dealt with it in some calmer fashion.* He was not in any way condoning the actions or failures of the guilty party, he simply felt that anger should not have been displayed. Even if the extreme suspicion of sabotage were proven, Glenn put himself in my position and stated that it "wouldn't—for my [Glenn's] own protection—permit me to raise my voice about it. I would find another means, but I *would* take means." One is reminded of the oath he swore to himself as a child never again to lose his temper. A single element ties that situation to his current philosophy. He stated: "for my own protection" but I really think he meant "for my opponent's protection." As a child, he was afraid that he could do bodily harm; now at nearly forty, he has transformed that anxiety into a much more benevolent posture. His most recent thinking on the subject provided an interesting explanation of why anger was not appropriate.

He told the story of some distant acquaintance who had met his tragic end in an auto accident. The nature of

*Without half trying, anyone can unearth a sheaf of medical opinion that claims to relate the kind of emotional bondage advocated by Gould with incidences of high blood pressure, heart attack, and stroke.

the collision was such that it seemed to Glenn to be partially a result of the victim's lack of concentration at a crucial moment. Furthermore, Glenn discovered that the dead man had embarked on the fatal journey in the aftermath of a heated argument. This caused Gould to conclude that there was a direct causal relationship between the pre-trip argument and the ensuing tragedy.

And *this* was the reason that I was wrong to berate the incompetent technician; maybe I would upset him and he would have an auto accident. Please understand, this is not a humorous or flippant sequitur on my part, this was exactly what Gould said and this is what he believed. He continued: "Forgive me for sounding like an old-fashioned Methodist or something, but I think one really has to live one's life with a spiritual direction in mind and not a material direction." He went on, trying to convince me to see the light. "I maintain a sense of the right of every human being to make infinite error—even at my expense."

Contrast this statement with his actions. The transgressions of Paul Myers and other producers from whom Glenn shifted away over the years could hardly be characterized as "infinite error," but, nevertheless, that didn't prevent him from severing the relationship—hardly in keeping with this last avowal. Of course, this might be a trick statement, granting the *right* to commit error, but acting in retaliation nevertheless. More likely, it stands as another example of the dichotomy between words and deeds.

As if sensing Gould's license for slipshod work, the technicians who were employed to supply us with electronic devices seemed to take full advantage of the situation. As I continually took note of the low quality of work being turned out in Toronto on our behalf, and watched Gould's passive role in observing it, I began to wonder exactly what was going on. On the one hand, Glenn was paying for it all. Don't forget that he was paying to provide a studio facility of the highest quality—one in no way inferior to that which we could find within the walls of Columbia Records—and all of this electronic hardware was his personal property. On the other hand, I was not only representing the interests of the Masterworks Department but attempting to look after my own health as well. For example, the night that I have been describing had been long and tedious as a result of the technician's faults. Without question, that placed an additional burden upon me—way beyond what I could have reasonably expected.

So, one day, in our postrecording wind-down talks, I told him of my observations. I tried to make it clear that I felt that neither "Columbia Records" nor "Glenn Gould Limited" were entities that should tolerate this kind of slipshod work; we both deserved better. I went on to say that it almost appeared as though he were seeking to employ people of less than average competence.

This opened up a whole, unexpected, subject. Glenn then informed me that he didn't believe in the concept of "intelligence"; there was no such thing as a stupid man. Well, tired though I was, this kind of provocative statement could not go unchallenged. I strongly stated that there was indeed such a concept and that perhaps we had seen ample proof of it right there within the confines of our operation. Try as I might, I couldn't get him to budge. I invented illustrative stories where the central character was, by anyone's standards, "stupid." He wouldn't see it that way. The most I could extract from him was an admission that perhaps this person was in the wrong line of work. In other words, everyone was equally intelligent; it was just a matter of each one finding his niche of optimum productivity. By this reasoning, he had to admit that Glenn Gould wasn't a "better" piano player than Mr. X, he was merely lucky that he found the area of work he was destined for. Perhaps Mr. X would be happier as a plumber.

Around this time I became aware of a nuance in his vocabulary that had completely eluded me. Very often I would hear him refer to some third party as "a dear man."

These words had always seemed self-explanatory to me and I never thought to look beneath the surface of their meaning. But little by little it began to dawn on me, as the evidence accumulated, that the words "a dear man" were euphemistic for what I would describe as "a sad, unintelligent man." Sometimes the phrase was "a very dear man," and this emphasis checked out in my own interpretation as well. Story after story told by Gould started to take on a new meaning. Soon I realized that it wasn't that Glenn couldn't recognize the quality I would name "stupidity," he simply wouldn't give it that title—so he invented a substitute.

Of course, he couldn't admit to this use of euphemism, for to do so would undermine his whole theory of IQ equality. But consistent observation of his use of the term (after the light had dawned) convinced me without question that it was so. In the midst of all this, I suddenly remembered an incident that had taken place several years before, in New York.

We were in the middle of a recording session at the 30th Street studio and had reached the point where we were listening to the tapes in order to plan our rough splicing strategy. The whole technique of the "instant playback" for making custom-fitted inserts did not really come into being until we moved our activities to Toronto, so we were less sure of the compatibility of takes. As our story opens, a particular juxtaposition of performances had been settled upon, but we really had no absolute proof that tempos would match. Under these circumstances, the best thing to do is to concoct a kind of rough test splice by using two tape recorders, each one loaded with one of the two takes that were going to be "test fit" together. First, the change-over point is decided upon. Next, the machine holding the take that will be heard first is backed up about thirty seconds before the switching point. Then the other machine (holding the take that will be heard after the switch) is carefully cued so that it will begin playing this second take at precisely the right place in the music. Finally the plan is put into action. The first machine starts to play the material from the first take. When the splice point is reached, the first machine is stopped and the second machine is started so the new material can be heard. Although far from satisfactory from a polished engineering point of view, the exercise does provide the closest possible linkage of the two performances (short of actually cutting them together on the spot) and certainly reveals the answer to the question of tempo. We were to do experiments like this many times over in Toronto. However, in New York, a third party was involved—one of the two union engineers. This man had jurisdiction over all the physical operations aside from picking the exact point of conjunction and cuing the change-over, both of which fell into the producer's domain.

So I told Glenn to wait a few moments while we set up the experiment, and then we would play it for him. I went to join the engineer, and together we cued up the appropriate takes for the test. The physical actions required of the tape machine operator are sometimes a bit awkward, especially if the starting and stopping of the recorders must be accompanied by simultaneous switching of audio channels at the point of the change-over. As it happened, on the first attempt to demonstrate the test splice for Gould, the engineer missed his cue and the trick didn't work. Gould, who by now was impatient, jumped from his chair and, erroneously thinking that somehow I had incorrectly cued the engineer, ran over to where we were preparing to repeat the demonstration, held up his hand with extended first finger (in the characteristic "stand-by" gesture of someone ready to deliver a physical "cue"), and said to me, a bit condescendingly: "Here, let the master do it!" Well, at the time I remember thinking that I had two choices: The one I didn't take would have probably done wonders for reducing my workload. The one I chose was to draw another of those deep breaths, step aside, and let Glenn cue the engineer.

$$\bullet \quad \bullet \quad \bullet$$

Back to Toronto. After I had remembered the above story, I waited for an appropriate place in Glenn's "All Men Are Created Equal" speech to remind him of that New York incident. My opportunity soon came and, in the least threatening tone I could muster, I brought up the event. We had never spoken about this before, so I'm sure that my recollection of the story must have been surprising to Gould. He listened to it and then immediately broke in with: "No, no, sir . . . you must be wrong . . . I could never have said something like that!" But, in fact, he had. The original incident was not a little bothersome to me, and there was no doubt about his exact words.

I don't think I really expected him to own up to that phrase spoken in New York, but I was curious to watch him try to squirm out of it. However, the thing that emerged most significantly from the experience was that just as the young Glenn had witnessed the momentary eruption of violent feelings within him, I had witnessed at 30th Street a momentary exposure of what I really believe were his true convictions. He *was* the master of piano playing. He wanted to deny it, but the phrase accidentally popped out in relation to recording techniques—about which I was, and still am, unwilling to acknowledge his superiority over me.

In retrospect, it is tempting to align this anecdote with the fact that Glenn Herbert Gould wrote at least three articles for *High Fidelity* magazine in 1965 under one of his favorite pseudonyms: Dr. Herbert von Hochmeister. *Hochmeister,* of course, literally translates from the German as "high master."

Earlier I referred to the fact that Glenn once acted in the capacity of producer for the recording of another pianist. This activity took place in 1973, the artist was Antonin Kubalek, and his repertoire consisted of some works of Erich Korngold. Initially Glenn was to share the duties as coproducer with another man named Tony Thomas, but by the time they got down to writing a contract, Gould had elevated his own title to producer, while demoting Thomas to some sort of associate status.

Following the recording sessions, Gould discussed the project with me and wasted no time in saying that he thoroughly enjoyed the experience and that I could be sure that it would not be the last time he would indulge in that activity, although to the best of my knowledge, Glenn never repeated the endeavor. He went on to say that what he relished most was the feeling of power that came from pressing the talk-back button and saying "Take one!" I questioned him at length about this feeling, and he further related that as he was actually doing it, he expressed the opinion to someone nearby that "Andy Kazdin really has a most enjoyable profession." I tried to tell him that, in fact, I derived no pleasure whatsoever from the rather functional act of calling out take numbers and that I would gladly give it up altogether if some trustworthy mechanical process were invented to replace my voice. He was surprised by this and said: "I would have assumed that's what a producer would have enjoyed most."

When I think of the enormous process involved in seeing a record through to final release and I realize what a minuscule sliver of that process is actually apparent at the recording session, and then try to assess the tiny fraction of *that* activity consumed by saying "Take one," it casts a rather pathetic light on Gould's naïve, childish statement that we should enjoy a sense of power in the insignificant act of slating takes. Aspiring to this portion of the producer's duties is exactly parallel to a child's wanting to be a fireman when he grows up so he can ride on a Big Red Truck. Recalling Glenn's fantasy of conducting war maneuvers from an isolated room, it suggests that in this case he had somehow confused "Take one!" with "Fire one!"

But the important aspect of this story is the central concept of the quest for power. It seems a little out of line with Gould's self-proclaimed attitude of equality among all men. Once, when learning about the unfortunate demotion of someone he knew in a New York corporation, he expressed to me his sincere sorrow over the incident and said: "My anticapitalistic feeling at this moment comes out in an especially strong way because I sort of try to visualize the emotional strain on someone like M—— who is very position-conscious, I would think, from what little I've seen of him." He went on to clarify that his ultimate fear was that the emotional strain would cause some kind of coronary problem—always his imagined nemesis. Again, the question must be asked whether the self-revelations made during the Kubalek experience—including the reshaping of his official title—really tally with this apparent concern for his fellow man.

Glenn claimed to be an avowed socialist and would spend hours of conversation berating the capitalistic system. He would explain at length that an individual was wrong to pursue corporate advancement and the financial increments that went with it if, indeed, he really didn't need the extra money. He would repeatedly say: "That's what is wrong with your country" while trying to convince me that the seeking of monetary rewards is, spiritually, an unworthy goal. Yet it didn't take the debating expertise of a William F. Buckley to unearth, and confront him with, countless points of discrepancy between what he professed and what he actually did. Just mention the whole question of recording artist's royalties—an area that seemed to obsess him—and he would quickly crumble and sheepishly explain that you had pointed quite accurately to a flaw in his argument. With little or no prodding, he would admit that his espousal of socialism and equality as a lifestyle was a theoretical argument—one that he fervently wished to adhere to—but, of course, being human, his weakness caused him to succumb to the pleasures of capitalism, power, and the rest.

In almost every conversation directly relating to a recording, he would use the word *we* when describing activities that took place. For example: "We started to record at seven forty-five Saturday night"—a very proper use of the word, or "That's the place where we decided to use take three"—an improper use, as the only person ever to make decisions about what takes to use was Gould himself. Now, I don't believe that this had anything to do with the "royal we." There were plenty of times when he said "I" when he meant it. But in relation to this supposedly collegial endeavor (Gould and Kazdin making a recording) he persisted in retroactively "sharing" every decision with me when clearly he had made the artistic ones unilaterally. I believe this was done in the spirit of trying to "include" me in all aspects of the project so as not to be blunt in exposing the fact that, from an artistic point of view, Gould was running the show all by himself.

In a way, he was in error here if he thought that he somehow needed to "handle me with kid gloves." I knew better than anyone his very special concern for the performance he recorded and felt absolutely no assault on my ego in letting him make the artistic decisions. There was plenty for me to do on his albums from a technical point of view so as to secure my emotional involvement in our product. I never felt for a moment (with Gould or any other artist I produced) that it was necessary for me to insert myself into the interpretive aspect of the recording. If I was asked a question about the performance, I would candidly give my opinion, but unless the artist sought my advice, I stayed away from that subject. Gould demanded this "invisible" role of his producers, and, perhaps, it was my dedication to the same principle that helped secure our working relationship for fifteen years. However, Glenn must have constantly wrestled with the questions of superiority and equality for he found it necessary to oil his spoken phrases with this salutary "we." The ironic fact is that in this regard, I would have been most happy to "Let the master do it."

It is a bit curious that "the master," to the best of my knowledge, never taught any students; at least not individually. He may have lectured at the university level in his younger years, but he never accepted any private pupils who wanted to improve their command of piano playing. Actually, this was not surprising because Gould's chief assets as a pianist were his phenomenal technique and his remarkable insights into the structure of the music he performed. These last perceptions cannot be taught to anyone who doesn't already have them, and the whole issue of technique was a very sensitive one for him. Glenn made it extremely clear to me that he didn't want to discuss this subject, and he explained his reluctance by retelling the tale of the spider and the centipede. For those not familiar with the story, it goes like this:

Once upon a time there was a spider who sought to catch a centipede in order to devour her. But no matter how hard the spider tried, the centipede, aided by the speed afforded by her many legs, was always able to outrun her predator. Then one day, the spider came upon the centipede sunning herself on a large rock, and a plan formed in his crafty brain.

After slowly approaching the rock, the spider stopped at a safe distance—just as the centipede became aware of the imminent danger. But before the prey could run, the spider began talking: "Oh, lovely Centipede, don't run. Please listen to what I have to say. I will stay here, far away, but you must answer one question for me. For days now I have been pursuing you with no success due to your magnificent grace and speed. I am a mere spider with but a few legs and you, clever Centipede, have one hundred. I marvel at the control and coordination you display whenever you move. It is all I can do to keep track of my six legs, how do you manage to control one hundred? Please tell me, I implore, which one do you move first? Is it number forty-five? Do you then follow with number seventy-three? What comes next? Is it eighty-two? or fifty-nine? Perhaps number thirteen follows number twenty-two, or is it sixty-one?"

For the first time in her life, the centipede began to ponder these questions about a feat that had always been performed by instinct. The more she thought, the more confused she became. Suddenly the spider lunged toward her, but the centipede's conscious thoughts could not maneuver the hundred legs that instinct had controlled so smoothly, and she remained motionless, completely paralyzed—and the spider finally landed his quarry.

So many times was this story referred to that Glenn coined an expression to indicate that its lessons were applicable to the subject of the moment. "Ah . . . sir . . . I'm afraid that that's one of those *centipedal* questions." He was trying to indicate that there were certain areas that he didn't even want to think about, much less discuss. I believe he felt that his remarkable tactile facility was a kind of mysterious gift that he neither completely understood nor was willing to question. Perhaps his fear was that if, like the centipede, he began to analyze the process, he would become paralyzed by his intellectual dissection and lose the ability.

So he certainly did not wish to teach any students and declined to talk about the subject at all. Once, however, he began to make cautious "wide circles" around the forbidden topic, and I sensed that he was a bit more receptive than usual to some carefully worded questions. He had just made the remark that, having recently listened to a Vladimir Horowitz recording, he could not fathom how someone of the Russian pianist's vast reputation could possibly be as ill-equipped from the standpoint of technique as Glenn judged him to be. This was a very provocative statement to make, and I tried to get him to enlarge on the subject.

First, he had to make it clear that the way in which

he defined *technique* was a bit different from what one naturally thinks of when hearing the word. Normally, when a pianist is credited as having a "good technique," the critic is saying that the performer's fingers are capable of moving over his instrument with abundant velocity, control, and accuracy. While Glenn certainly acknowledged that these qualities are included in his own definition, to him "technique" was a far more all-encompassing notion that referred to the performer's whole approach—mental and physical—to making music.

One of the rather amorphous concepts he tried to convey was that when he played, he kept a mental image of every key on the piano—not only where each note was, but how it would feel to reach for it and touch it. Once that process (strictly mental) had been accomplished, it was a rather simple matter actually to strike the key with the desired force. In this way, he held the concept of technique to include both parts of the process—the mental preparation and the physical execution. I remember this conversation with him vividly, chiefly because we never probed the subject as deeply at any other time.

His description brought to mind a scene I had remembered from a movie called *Little Big Man*. The hero is being instructed how to perfect his ability at sharpshooting. His teacher, a girl with remarkable marksmanship, is trying to convey the essence of her technique by stressing the importance of concentrating on what is about to take place before actually firing the pistol. She says that her student must learn to "draw, and shoot that bottle *before* you touch the gun." It seemed to me that if I had understood anything that Glenn had said, then this movie scene provided a perfect parallel. I told him the sharpshooting story and asked if this was the same thing he was saying about the piano. He replied "Exactly." Then he quickly indicated that he would rather change the subject. Those far more knowledgeable about this than I have suggested that this concept is very similar to the teachings of Zen. If true, then it is fascinating to contemplate that

that term was never spoken in all the years of our acquaintance. Another secret life? . . .

Glenn had mentioned on more than one occasion that it was not necessary for him to practice several hours a day (or at all) in order to be able to play in good form. As usual, this kind of flamboyant statement provided a fertile area for discussion because practically all instrumentalists state that without the necessary arduous daily practice hours, their "technique" will suffer. As usual, I tried to test the strength of his conviction by concocting more and more extreme examples in order to observe his reactions. Eventually I understood that he was really saying that although he practiced to discover the musical problems (and their solutions) associated with the new piece he was learning, it was, in fact, completely unnecessary to the proper functioning of his fingers.

Still somewhat skeptical about the physical effects of not practicing, I told him that when I used to play timpani in orchestras, I was able to exist from day to day without extra practice—as long as I performed on a more or less steady schedule. However, if I had no contact with the instrument for any extended period, when I first started to play again I would become aware immediately of my limited physical endurance. For example, I would try to play an extended rapid passage and find that my hands would develop cramps and not be able to maintain control. Only by "keeping in shape" would I continue to possess the muscle tone necessary to support any such extended effort. He interrupted my story. "Yes, but if you could completely relax . . . soak your hands in hot water and take a tranquilizer, you would find that you could play without cramps—and without practicing!"

Of course, these recommendations were not really designed for the timpanist; they were, in fact, the steps Gould himself always took before playing. The hand-soaking was a "must." At Eaton's, he discovered that the water from the hot-water tap did not have a high enough temperature, so he brought in an electric tea kettle. At appropriate moments throughout the session, he would announce that it was time "to go soak," and this meant heating a kettle of water to the boiling point, going into a lavatory to use a small sink, and immersing his hands until he was ready to resume recording. When he went back to the piano, his fingers were beet red. How he could withstand the burning effect of the water heated to such a high temperature, I do not know.

The plain fact was that his ability to navigate the most difficult passages on the piano was so extraordinary that I, for one, was completely unwilling to question where the technique came from. Maybe it was the soaking, maybe it was his "chair," maybe the tranquilizers, maybe just plain talent—whatever it was, no one was going to pooh-pooh the peculiar rituals he engaged in before performing his miracles.

Perhaps because it was the most visible symbol of Gould's eccentric approach to the piano, a lot has been written about "The Chair." A quick summary of the publicized information would include the following facts:

1. Gould was happy playing the piano only if he could use his own, special piano chair.
2. This chair was built considerably lower than conventional seats and, because of that, offered Gould the characteristically low approach to the instrument that was vital to his technique.
3. The chair was in very bad repair. In fact, it was the "swing and sway" aspect of its instability that Gould found irreplaceable.
4. At some time in the deep past, thinking that it would be a welcome donation, people at Columbia Records secretly took measurements and built an exact replica of the chair. Gould tried it, and finding that it was solidly constructed without the "give" he required, smiled graciously, but discarded the gift and continued to use the old original.

5. The rickety condition of the chair caused it to emit creaks and snaps as he moved in it, and few Gould recordings are exempt from this percussion obbligato.
6. The chair folded up and fitted inside of its own wooden suitcase, so it could accompany Gould to whatever location required his services.

To the best of my knowledge, all of these points are true. In fact, the only one to which I personally was not an eyewitness is number 4. In addition, I can add an amusing chronology that will underline Gould's dependency on this unusual piece of furniture.

As originally conceived, the chair consisted of a wooden frame that was hinged in such a way as to allow it to fold into a more or less flat configuration so that it could be stored in its box. When open for use, the top of the frame provided a four-sided rim for supporting the actual cushioned seat. In addition, this square opening was bisected (front to back) by a narrow wooden crossbeam that was designed to offer more support to the seat and user.

The seat itself consisted of a square plywood panel—of dimensions just larger than the hole it would surmount—upon which was placed some soft cushiony material. The whole was covered with a kind of plastic or leatherette fabric that kept it all together.

Now, over the years, the following metamorphoses took place:

1. Somehow, the cushioned panel got separated (if it ever was firmly attached) from the frame. This merely meant that Gould had to center it by eye each time he set up the device for use.
2. Perhaps it was the friction caused by the separation that began to wear out the underside of the leatherette where it wrapped around the wood panel and was tacked in place.
3. Eventually a loose flap was created that allowed the stuffing to come out and be discarded.

4. For a long time, the seat unit consisted of only the plywood panel rather loosely covered by the leatherette cover—no stuffing was left at all.

5. The ravages of time and motion eventually began to cause little splits around the perimeter of the wood panel. Soon pieces began to chip away, thus reducing the dimensions of the board. It was during this period that the audio content of the chair as a whole was at its peak.

6. When the size of the wood panel became smaller than the dimensions of the supporting frame, the board acted more as a liability than an asset (I'm sure there's a pun in there somewhere!) because it now functioned as a teeter-totter, fulcrummed as it was by the bisecting center strut. The wood was discarded.

7. In the end (another pun?) the chair as a hole (I couldn't resist) consisted of the wooden frame, over which was draped—as in a kind of ritualistic symbolism—the thin remains of the leatherette cover.

Doubtless the reader has noticed that nowhere in this history has there been any mention of Glenn's reaction to the deterioration of the seat. It must be understood that in the final analysis, his gluteus maximus was positioned directly over an open rectangle—made even more treacherous by the center strut, which, I must reiterate, ran from front to back. The reason I have omitted any mention of his personal trauma is because I don't know of any. I never once witnessed any increasing displeasure with the chair's comfort as its luxury decreased. A really clever psychologist could gleefully cross-reference this to the question of the piano as mistress.

Chief among his noticeable physical accouterments was his scarf and gloves. The latter, obviously, were in place to keep his hands from being cold. We have learned that his ability at the piano was dependent, to some degree, on his hands' being warm—or downright hot. Of course, the gloves offered such a cumbersome restraint to the rapid movement required of his fingers that it was not possible for him to perform at peak efficiency while actually wearing them. Therefore, despite the photograph on the cover of this book showing the young, gloved Gould sitting at the instrument, it is a bit of a mystery to me how the notion got publicized that he wore gloves while actually recording. In all the years of our association, I never witnessed this extraordinary condition.

The scarf, on the other hand, was a different matter. It was designed to shelter his neck and shoulders from drafts. We have all been told by our parents that we should protect ourselves from these silent yet deadly invaders that are always present to cause colds and stiffness. Scientifically speaking, all a draft can do is create a drop in temperature of the exposed area. Admittedly, this coldness might not be comfortable and could lead to more serious physical ailments, but I have never been able to comprehend why "drafts" were bad, while there was nothing wrong with standing outside in the Canadian winter. It really seemed to be governed by the fictitious rule that "Cold air outdoors is okay, but cold air indoors is to be feared."

Perhaps even more widely noticed than Gould's chair was his singing. He once said that perhaps the vocal accompaniment was an indication of how he would really like his phrases at the piano to be made. This was as good an explanation as I ever heard from him as to what his singing represented in the totality of his music making. In any case, it was omnipresent when he played. Gould told me that he was not in any way "proud" of these sounds and was not pleased that they infiltrated his recordings; he just couldn't do anything to stop them.

Naturally, we all applied ourselves to the problem of devising some technical trick to keep the singing out of the microphones, but this was not a simple task. The producer and engineer were almost doomed to failure before they began because there was only one sure way to shield the mikes from a direct-line pickup of his voice while not in any way preventing a normal, open reproduction of the piano: Place a box over Gould's head. Even a more complex and less humorous version of this—a kind of booth that would include the whole of Gould and just the keyboard and pedals of the piano—would not work in practice because Glenn had to hear the sounds his instrument was producing as he played. We eventually came up with a compromise solution that involved erecting a large, sound-absorbent screen just to Glenn's right that partially shielded the microphones from an uninterrupted view of his face. It worked a little bit, and it certainly didn't hurt.

I discovered an interesting fact in relation to my own perception of the singing. I found I really was able to "tune it out" and had to keep reminding myself of its presence in order to be aware of it. I didn't consciously try to suppress these sounds from my hearing, they just faded into the background when I concentrated on the music.

From time to time, consumers would complain about these noises (reviewers and critics had long since given up commenting and learned to live with them). One letter sticks in my mind above all others. It was written by a lady living somewhere in the Midwest, and it began by explaining that she had just come home from her local record store where she had purchased the first volume of the French suites. In her second paragraph, one could sense the lowering of her voice—the way someone imparts a great secret—and she said: "Now, you're not going to believe this . . . but . . . someone is singing in the background as Mr. Gould is playing!" I wrote back to her venturing the guess that this was probably her first Glenn Gould album. I explained the situation to her and also told how I'd been able to ignore it. I concluded with the hope that she'd learn to overlook the singing in favor of the really remarkable music making that was going on at the same time. She never wrote back. I guess she learned.

5

One of the many sad things about Gould's untimely death was the fact that the series of seven keyboard concertos by Bach would never be completed. When we began our association, two of them had already been recorded; number 1 had been performed with Leonard Bernstein, but it existed only as a monophonic disc, and number 5 had been taped in stereo with Vladimir Golschmann. As any Bach work Gould played had a higher sales potential than recordings Glenn might make of other composers' music, and as it was felt at Masterworks that, in general, concerto recordings had a higher sales potential than solo piano discs, it followed that it was desirable to record the Bach keyboard concertos played by Glenn Gould. Glenn and I were both told that we should waste no time in continuing the series.

Our first project in following this mandate required reenlisting the services of Golschmann and recording concertos number 3 and number 7. These, combined with the old number 5, made our first release. Then, several years later, we once again collaborated with Golschmann and recorded number 2 and number 4; this became volume 2. Our plan—unfortunately never realized—was to eventually re-record number 1 in stereo and add to it the missing number 6. We already knew that we would have to seek another conductor because in the interim, Vladimir Golschmann had passed away.

The two collaborations with Golschmann were a joy, both for me and for Glenn. From Gould's point of view, Golschmann was ideal in that he had full command of the orchestra but, at the same time, allowed Glenn to shape the interpretation to his own design. His wry sense of humor made him particularly charming. We taped these concertos in the 30th Street studio and I recall that after one of the sessions we three were sharing a taxicab uptown and Golschmann was talking enthusiastically about what they had just accomplished. He looked at Glenn and with apparent seriousness said: "I want to tell you how much I enjoyed this recording. Please keep in mind always that if no other conductor will go into the studio with you, *I* will go!"

A gentleman of his accomplishments is made even more likable by the irresistible trait of not taking himself too seriously. He used to prove this occasionally by asking us if we liked his "immortal downbeat." These words stuck in my mind, and once I had the opportunity to reply to him in kind. Shortly after one of the volumes of Bach concertos was released, I received a delightful letter from Golschmann, addressing me as Mr. Kazdin, in which he asked if it would be possible for him to purchase some additional copies of the record "at a friendly price." I knew what that meant (and so did Golschmann). Columbia Records always made it possible for its recording artists to purchase copies of their own records at a substantial discount, and, of course, this courtesy was extended to Golschmann. I wrote back to him describing the cost involved and concluded with: "So, if you would kindly apply your Immortal Downbeat to a check for $42.50, I will send you the copies you requested." Practically by return mail I received his reply. No more Mr. Kazdin. This time it was: "Mon cher Ami! It *is* Immortal, isn't it!"

After the splicing of the concertos was complete, it was time to do the mixing, and here the question of musical balances became an important issue. This is not a new problem for any record producer. Basically, there are two forces at play: the opinion of the producer and the opinion of the soloist. It sounds silly and childish, but my experience has convinced me that the following is almost universally true, regardless of the personalities involved. As if to compensate for years of concertizing where he had no control over the volume of the orchestra, if the soloist is asked to participate in the decision of balance, he will invariably choose a ratio that is tilted toward his own playing in an unrealistically high proportion.*

I remember having to handle a situation that took place years before the Bach concertos. It concerned a recording on which a first-chair player from a symphony orchestra performed a concerto for his instrument. Just after the splicing was finished, I invited him to come into our editing room and listen to the performance in order to approve my choice of takes. After he had listened and made his observations, he asked: "Now, that's not going to be the balance on the record, is it?" I explained that we had not yet done the mixing operation at which time that issue would be definitively resolved, but I certainly was interested in his thoughts on the subject. I told him that the sound of his instrument was on a separate track and we had a pretty wide choice of options when balancing commenced. He said that, at the moment, his track was being reproduced at too low a volume and he hoped that when the time came, I would remedy the situation. I

---

*I can think of one notable exception. Perhaps because his early training was as a conductor (in fact, he recorded all the Mozart piano concertos, directing from the keyboard), Murray Perahia envisions a balance between soloist and orchestra that is realistic and correct.

said that I would be happy to take a few minutes right then to discover his desired balance. I suggested that we play back the tape again, and for him to instruct the engineer to manipulate the track levels until he was satisfied. He agreed, and we rewound the tape back to the beginning. In those early days of multi-track recording, we were dealing only with three (today the numbers can go as high as thirty-two). The orchestra was divided between two tracks—left and right, and the soloist had a track to himself that would eventually be positioned in the center of the stereo "picture."

So, the playback began and our visiting instrumentalist started to gesture to the engineer in order to indicate what adjustments should be made. A little more solo, a little less orchestra. Just a little *more* solo, a little *less* orchestra. I stood silently at the side of the room so I could observe the positions of the engineer's level controls. Eventually the musician proclaimed that the balance was satisfactory. I looked down at the mixing console and the engineer caught my eye and moved his hands out of the way so I could clearly see his controls. What I saw was the soloist's track raised to the maximum position that the console would allow and the two orchestral tracks reduced to the point that, it was fair to say, they had been effectively turned off.

When the recording was originally made, naturally the producer desired that the sounds recorded on the three tracks would leave sufficient options for final balance adjustments when the postproduction mixing took place. This meant that a certain degree of isolation was afforded to the soloist. However, in a more or less natural-sounding environment, the soloist was not subjected to the extreme case of isolation—being put in a soundproof booth. Besides making it rather difficult for the musician to hear his one hundred colleagues, the situation really did not require such a drastic operation. Therefore, if one were to audition the soloist's track alone, one could hear that some sounds of the orchestral accompaniment had "leaked" into his microphone. This soft orchestral leakage and the bigger-than-life image of the soloist himself was what we were now listening to in the editing room, and this was the balance of the two forces that he felt should be heard on the record. Well, we might ask, why not? This was the ratio of solo to orchestra that he was used to, as his instrument was only inches from his ears. The fact that the recording had been effectively converted from stereo to mono by his balance choice did not disturb him in any way. I thanked him for his time and bid him good day. Then I set about the task of making a balance that would more properly represent the impression that someone in the audience would have had.

I've seen countless examples of this myopic view of concerto balances in the years that followed, and it always fell to the producer to summon all his tact and talk the soloist into something realistic. It just so happens that at the completion of the splicing of the first volume of Bach concertos, Gould was in New York and I invited him in to listen to the performance. Before I knew it, *déjà vu* was upon me. We were going through a repeat of the previous story, but Glenn was being a little more realistic than the orchestral player. Perhaps he had greater experience in listening to himself as soloist on concerto recordings (he had, by that time, performed on six records in this way) than the other musician. Nonetheless, the balance he caused the engineer to make was not really satisfactory for record release. I told him I would do the best I could when the mixing came about, but secretly I was worried. One of the things that saved me was the fact that Glenn had asked us to make a tape copy of the concertos in the "Gould balance" right after he had created it. He wanted to take something back to Toronto to play and revel in. A few days later I got a call from him admitting that he had "perhaps gone a bit too far" with the prominence of the piano and that he thought it would be okay if I reduced it somewhat.

Eventually he heard the completed balance and had

more comments to make. I have always believed that if some tragedy would have prevented Gould from ever playing the piano again, I would have recommended, as his career counselor, that he go immediately into the field of professional debating. Being on the other side of the table when Glenn wanted to convince you of something was no fun! He could pull out more plausible rationales per minute than anyone else I knew. Now, here he was trying to coerce me into increasing the volume of his instrument on this concerto recording. First, the piano was not loud enough during his solos when the orchestra merely accompanied him; then the piano was not loud enough in the sections where the orchestra had to play the thematic material and he had merely to accompany them. Each of these requests came complete with a convoluted series of rationales, but the final outcome was simply: more piano.

We never reached blows on the subject, but I was so firmly convinced that my mix represented a realistic balance while his conception was motivated simply by ego (elaborately cloaked in specious logic, as only Gould could concoct) that I brought the problem to my superior at Columbia Masterworks, John McClure. He listened to the recording and agreed to speak with Glenn on the subject. Not too long thereafter, Gould was again in town and the three of us convened in McClure's office. We listened through the concertos again. John had to endure Glenn's "playback performance" wherein the pianist conducts the recording, makes occasional remarks to tell you how great the playing is, and generally presents his audience with the difficult task of concocting, on the spot, an astronomical number of variations on the thought: "Glenn, there is no doubt that this is the best recording of ——— ever made and you are fantastic in it." As Gould's recording career progressed, his ego enlarged to match. There was a time when, while listening to playbacks at our editing studios, if a well-wisher would drop by to say hello, linger for a moment to listen to whatever Gould was working on, and proffer a compliment such as "That's really beautiful," Glenn would reply, "Oh, thank you very much." As time progressed, the comment "That's really beautiful" would elicit the answer, "Yes, I know."

After McClure was treated to an audiovisual presentation of the Bach concertos, we had to come to grips with Gould's complaint. In all the years of our acquaintance, John McClure performed two services for me that I will never forget: (1) he hired me at Columbia Records in the first place, and (2) he defended my musical balances of Gould's Bach concertos. The latter might not seem so significant, but in the mercurial world of the record business, where artistic temperament is very often allowed to exert itself successfully, the simple act of supporting a colleague in favor of an artist is a rare thing. Over the years, so many producers have been "sold down the river" that they had to obtain commutation tickets and boat paddles.

One other issue bothered Gould about the concertos: "reverberation." Because the sessions had taken place in a recording studio rather than in a large auditorium, it had been necessary to add some artificial reverberation to the tapes when the mixing took place. This was done to give the piano and the orchestra the same kind of ambience that a more spacious recording location would have afforded. Glenn found it pleasing in relation to the orchestra but objectionable when applied to the piano. Here his logic was extremely persuasive. He said, "You're aware that my style of performance in Bach involves using a very staccato articulation. Do you know how difficult that is to execute and maintain? Please, after all my effort, don't undo that for me by tying all my notes together with reverberation!" He won the point. I returned to the editing room and remixed the "outer" movements of the concertos with no reverberation added to the piano. We had agreed that the electronic enhancement was not really a liability in the slow movements, therefore a reasonable compromise had been reached. If removing the slight reverberation from the piano track was the "price" I had to pay for retaining a realistic, objective balance between piano and orchestra, it was certainly worth it.

A quaint example of "give-and-take" Gould style (that is, you'd give and he'd take) came up regarding an article he had written for *High Fidelity* magazine in August 1975, but this story really starts some years before. In one of our more relaxed conversations, I was describing for him an interesting psychological effect that I had observed in dealing with many recording artists over a considerable period of time. It went like this: After the recording sessions, it was usually the job of the producer to select the sequence of takes that would be spliced together to yield the final product. Some performers liked being a part of this process, and their involvement could run the gamut from a few casual suggestions given to the producer before beginning the task, or a desire to be present during the actual choosing (and making recommendations as it progressed), to the extreme position of wanting to undertake the entire job alone—as Gould did. All of these options would have been acceptable to any producer I know because the more the artist was involved, the more the producer was sure that the editing job would be deemed satisfactory.

Most likely, the procedure would consist of the artist and producer going through the takes together. If done thoroughly, this is a very painstaking task involving repeated listening and comparing to assure the artist that the best material is being selected for inclusion in the final recording. After the plan is solidified and the actual splicing is completed, the artist can be supplied with a tape copy of the composite in order to assess the final results, much in the same way in which Gould listened to his masters on the telephone. One difference occurs because Glenn was satisfied to hear it once via long-distance phone. Other artists generally play the tape they have received over and over.

Now it sometimes happens that despite the best efforts of everyone concerned, an occasional smudged note or some other minor defect managed to pass unnoticed during the original selection process. Possibly, while the offending element is being corrected, the artist might be present during the search of the alternative takes. While these "out-takes" are being perused, I have frequently observed the performer focusing his attention on some other—undisputed—musical phrase. When questioned about his interest, he would often reply: "Now that I hear it again, maybe take six is a better basic performance than the one we chose."

Chances are that take six was in no way better—it was just different. That is, in the intervening weeks, the musician had heard the same edited performance so many times that when an alternative—any alternative—was presented to him by accident, the differences that he heard (for good or for bad) made it sound fresher in some way, and hence preferable. The only solution to this was for the producer to summon all his patience and once again lead the artist through all the possible choices and show by careful comparison that they had indeed picked the superior take.

So often had I seen this effect in operation that I had dubbed it: "The Grass Is Always Greener in the Out-Takes" which I felt was a fitting description of the situation. Well, I told all this to Glenn, who smiled and, as I was to subsequently discover, tucked it all away for future reference.

A few years later, Glenn had agreed with *High Fidelity* magazine to do an article on the subject of splicing musical performances for commercial record release. This is always an interesting topic that tends to divide any group of musicians or record buyers rather sharply. Gould too had strong opinions on the subject, and the thrust of his article was that splicing was always a positive tool, if well executed. In fact, the unique feature of his piece was that it was preceded by an extremely interesting bit of "lab work." Glenn had done a series of listening experiments with a variety of people who had provided statistics to prove his case. While I enjoyed reading his article when I received my copy of the magazine, I was a little nonplussed by its title: "The Grass Is Always Greener in the Out-Takes." During some future conversation, I steered the subject around to the magazine piece. We had long since discussed his listening tests and their significance (I had always agreed with his premise), but this was my first opportunity to compliment him on the finished article. After having done so, I brought up the subject of the title and suggested to him in a humorous way that he "owed me royalties" for using my idea. To this day I don't believe I fully understand his answer. It was: "Ah, yes . . . well . . . you see, we authors don't mind digging through old garbage cans for our ideas." I still wonder: Was this simply a way of telling me that he felt that all was fair in love, war, and the composition of catchy titles for magazine articles, or was he, rather offensively, describing the fruits of my creation?

In a whimsical sense, the situation was reversed about a year later. In the autumn of 1976, I was honored to have a feature article about myself, illustrating the daily life of a classical record producer, published in the Sunday *New York Times*. The interviewer and author, Helen Epstein, spent several days accompanying me on my daily chores, attending recording sessions, editing sessions, and so on, in an effort to glean a typical picture of my activities. In order to enhance her story, she wanted to interview some of the recording artists with whom I worked on a regular basis. Helen hoped to be able to extract a sample from each interview that indicated what each of them felt was the value and function of a record producer in their individual approaches to the process of making records.

Toward this end, she spoke with E. Power Biggs, Pierre Boulez, and Glenn Gould. The first two provided her with interesting descriptions, and she was able to incorporate excerpts from their statements in her finished article. After she spoke with Glenn, however, she confided in me that she didn't come away with "good vibrations" and eventually decided not to quote him in the piece. This saddened me a little—not because of her decision (she proved to be a very sensitive writer and I trusted her feelings), but because of Glenn's attitude (whatever it was). The reader must understand that while I was delighted and proud to work with Biggs, Boulez, and many other artists, I had produced at least twice as many records with Glenn as with any other musician and had sustained a working relationship with him that lasted longer than any other as well. Although Helen referred to him in the article, I was sorry that she was not able to extract a usable quote from my prime "account."

Naturally, I tried to find out from her exactly what he had said. It seems that she found it difficult to keep him on the subject of "recording with a producer" rather than on the subject of Glenn Gould. The one quote that I still remember from this conversation was his remark that he found "any musical knowledge on the part of the producer unnecessary." I'm not quite sure what he really meant to say, but this is what he did say. Perhaps he was trying to indicate that during an actual recording session, he was not interested in hearing any musical opinions of his performance and certainly was not seeking advice of any kind. As referred to earlier, that attitude was uniquely Gould's and he never once felt any objection to it from me. Now that I think about it, he really didn't wish to hear opinions other than "that's great" at any time—before or after the sessions.

Clearly, if he would have just stopped and considered the long list of services I provided for him that someone with no formal education in music could never have performed, I'm sure he would not have made the remark. Paradoxically, it can be argued that the presence of a producer at a recording session is completely unnecessary. The musical artist and the recording engineer can achieve adequate results together if economics are not a factor. If the musician is willing to alternate his activities between playing and running into the control room to listen back and assess each take, the function of the producer is eliminated. However, if that musician happens to be the conductor of the New York Philharmonic and must spend half his time in the control room while his orchestra waits, the economics of the situation would surely sink the project. The plain fact is that Glenn, as well as all other recording artists, had gotten used to the convenience of a helpful musical presence on the other side of the glass window.

By pure coincidence, a mere three days after Helen Epstein's piece appeared in the *Times,* an article was printed in the *Toronto Globe and Mail* reporting on a recording session with the Toronto Symphony Orchestra and its talented young conductor, Andrew Davis, which I directed in Glenn's hometown. Of course, I knew that the author, John Kraglund, had been in attendance at the session, but I was not sure when his piece would be published. In fact, it was Glenn who first informed me of its appearance in print. He called me on the phone and kindly read the entire article. By that time he had seen the Epstein piece in the *Times* and undoubtedly had noticed the omission of his little talk with her—a fact that was never discussed between us. But now, with the Toronto paper before him, he told me several times on the phone that he felt that Kraglund had written a very good piece—much better than Helen Epstein's essay. The fact that the Kraglund interview quotes me as saying that "Glenn Gould is especially easy to work with. He knows what he wants and, especially important, he knows how to get it—which is not the case with many musicians" probably had nothing to do with Glenn's preference for the Canadian article.

I did not invent the expression "creative lying"—Glenn did. It was the way he rationalized any falsehoods he found it necessary to concoct. This should not be confused with the concept of the "white lie." If a harmless fiction is told because the truth would cause needless anguish to someone, that is a white lie. It is somehow considered acceptable (and merciful) to say that a lady's dress is "very becoming" when, indeed, it is not that at all and only serves as another bit of evidence confirming the continuing bad taste of the wearer.

However, if a lie is told in order to manipulate your fellow human being—you remember, all the people that are of equal intelligence—then, deep inside, it is a bit hard to think of your deed as being described by such words as *dishonest, cunning, Machiavellian,* or *conniving.* It is much better to adorn the process with a word that has never had a negative connotation: *creative.*

Over the years, I listened to Glenn plan how he was going to avoid talking to someone on the phone or in person. I saw him concoct elaborate schemes to help bring a personal relationship to an end. I watched the development of his second residence at the Four Seasons Hotel and the absurd stories he somehow got people to believe about why he was not living at home. It was impossible to observe all of this prevarication and not suspect that whenever he felt the situation warranted it, I too was being lied to—creatively, of course. Every time Gould canceled a recording session at the last minute, every time that his splicing instructions were not prepared in time to make the release schedule—in fact, every time that I listened to him give any kind of explanation for actions of his that were not exactly exemplary, I came to suspect that I was being treated to an exhibition of creative lying.

If the process can be summarized as the telling of whatever story is expedient in order to get your "opponent" to do what you want, then it surely is one of the most powerful tools in the process of control. After all, there is only a small difference between not telling the whole truth and telling direct lies. The kind of selective truth-telling that Gould practiced on everyone was, clearly, just another manifestation of creative lying. As practically every day of his life was spent carefully rationing the number of facts that he wished any one person to absorb, one can easily say that Glenn's whole existence was consumed with prevarication. This is not to imply that he was a pathological liar. Of course he wasn't. There is no suggestion here that he could not be trusted in general. I am simply positing that the "mystery man" image (in which no one person knows the whole Glenn Gould) cannot be flawlessly sustained without constant attention and constant fabrication. Some part of each day must be devoted to performing preventive maintenance on the subterfuge so that no leaks occur.

Therefore, it seems entirely fitting that these memoirs of our association be gathered together under the general banner of creative lying. Outside of his music making, it was his next most consuming passion. Why he found it necessary to live in a self-designed world of pseudo espionage and mock privacy can only be guessed at. Perhaps it was the ultimate form of game playing. If he had thought about it, would he really continue to pretend that Elisheva Kaufman was coming after him with a motive so unspeakable as to rationalize his crouching on the floor behind the locked (steel) door to my office? Hailed by many as the greatest living pianist, was it truly necessary for him to lust after the supposed "power" of saying "take one" at a recording session? In a way, all these traits indicate an immature, naïve outlook on life, and this is most certainly a paradox. On the one hand, his all-encompassing overview of musical form and style cannot be considered as anything other than the product of a highly developed artistic maturity. At the same time, he fantasizes that the way a husband should deal with the suspect reading tastes of his wife is to rip pages out of her magazine while she is asleep. He said it was "very effective." How could he possibly know?

For only a fleeting instant, it has crossed my mind that Gould was a kind of idiot savant, exhibiting genius-like knowledge and talents on one particular subject but evidencing subnormal intelligence everywhere else. I convinced myself that this could not be the case with him because his superior knowledge extended past the scope of music and reached into literature, philosophy, politics, and history. Still, even within the areas he excelled in, I would accidentally run into an "air pocket" of childish naïveté.

Once, when discussing a particular spot in a score he was recording, I asked him to focus for a moment on a measure that contained a *fermata*. This musical symbol instructs the performer to suspend the rhythmic pulse momentarily and "hold" a particular note (or rest) for a period of time longer than its mathematical value. The new duration is always left to the discretion of the player who, of course, must temper his decision with a knowledge of musical tradition, good taste, and common sense. In the particular case under discussion, I listened to Gould's performance and then asked if he was really honoring the *fermata* because (1) the note really seemed no longer than the basic notation would have indicated, and (2) the symbol was further enhanced by the composer's instruction (in Italian) *lunga*—long. As usual, my question was couched in such a way as to negate any possibility that I was advising him how to perform the piece, but rather as a simple check to see if, indeed, the instruction had been accidentally omitted from his printed score—or erroneously added to mine. He didn't take offense in any way. He confirmed that he did see the *fermata*, but with the addition of the word *lunga*, he minimized its musical effect. I said that I was a bit puzzled since *lunga* meant, if anything, to stretch the time interval, not abbreviate it. He acted surprised and commented that he had seen the word used before and always imagined that it translated as "lunge"—therefore, he speeded ahead. Even if he didn't know a word of Italian in general, or the commonly used musical terms in particular, one would think that a lifetime of listening to music and comparing its sound with the printed notation he saw in his scores would have given him an empirical feeling for the meaning of the word. But no, he invented his own scenario and definition. His command of the English language was sophisticated and colorful and yet, when referring to a motion picture, he would call it a "fillum."

On another occasion, we got into a rather extended conversation about the definition of the word *dinky*. It has always been my feeling (and Webster's, as well) that "dinky" meant small or insignificant. Glenn, on the other hand, used the word one day as a synonym for *nifty:* "The boy received a really dinky bicycle for his birthday." Where he picked that up I don't know, but I subsequently discovered an arcane British definition that does mean "smart" or "stylish." Perhaps it is unfair for me to criticize this usage until I fully understand the vestigial influence the United Kingdom has over Canada.

Errors of all sorts abounded in his life. In the fifth edition (1958) of *Baker's Biographical Dictionary of Musicians,* Gould's entry carried with it a rather humorous one. The last sentence reads: "Apart from his highly successful career as a concert pianist, Gould cultivates the jazz style of piano playing; he has given numerous exhibitions in the U.S. as an improviser with jazz groups; also composed jazz pieces." Now, anybody having the slightest acquaintance with Gould must have suspected that either this information was grossly incorrect, or that Glenn was leading some kind of Jekyll and Hyde existence; sneaking off in the dead of night, dark glasses in place, to participate in these jazz activities. In fact, he had neither the interest in nor the proclivity for this style of music.

When I brought the listing to Glenn's attention, he was only mildly bothered because he had already known of the error—it had been included in earlier editions of *Baker's.* His only comment was: "Oh, gosh, haven't they fixed that yet?" Apparently he had long since written to the editor of the dictionary to inform him of the mistake. He explained that what had probably happened in the first place was a confusion with the Austrian-born pianist

Friedrich Gulda, a man only two years Gould's senior who did indeed divide his attention between a concert career and jazz interests.

One thing about which there was no confusion was the piano that was suitable for Gould's unorthodox style of playing. When I began working with Glenn in the middle 1960s, he was using a Steinway piano that bore the identification number 318. This instrument had been carefully regulated to have the exact hair-trigger specifications that he required and, in addition, possessed a tone quality that provided him with no end of aesthetic pleasure. When a pianist reaches a certain stature in his career, one of the leading piano manufacturing companies often elects to provide him with an instrument for his major engagements at little or no charge. In return, the artist promises to perform on no other brand and, in so doing, grants the piano company the right to use his endorsement in their publicity. In these terms, Glenn was known as a "Steinway Artist." The normal procedure, before an impending concert, is for the pianist to visit the famous Basement at the New York office of Steinway & Sons where many pianos are stored (sort of like livestock before an auction) and, after playing on several, make his choice of which one will be delivered to his concert location.

In Glenn's case, having carefully worked on the innards of 318 to the point where it was tailored exactly to his needs, Steinway granted him the unique privilege of retaining sole control of its use—although they still owned it. Also, they reasoned, no one else would want to play the instrument in the peculiar condition that Glenn required, and converting it back and forth would be an enormous headache for all concerned. Not only was the instrument reserved for Gould's exclusive use, but it was permanently housed in one corner of Columbia Records' 30th Street studio. Don't forget that starting in early 1964, Gould gave up performing in front of concert audiences and needed a piano solely for the recording studio. Therefore, in a sense, Steinway was trading this seemingly generous gift of the piano's exclusive use for total relief from the "headache" of carting the instrument all over the country following the concert itinerary of the artist. It was kept locked at all times and everyone who worked there knew that it was the "Gould piano." When Glenn wanted to record, it was simply a matter of calling in a piano tuner to bring it into perfect condition.

Through all the years that we worked together in New York, 318 was the instrument used. When the decision was finally made to move our recording site to Toronto, Glenn personally paid for the shipping of the piano. As good luck would have it, Eaton's Department Store included a piano division that was an official Steinway dealer. This made them cordially receptive toward Gould's request that, between our sessions, 318 be stored backstage in their auditorium. Therefore, we were able to use that treasured instrument when we started working in Canada. In fact, not too long after, the complications of customs charges and other bureaucratic matters made it particularly difficult for Steinway in New York to rationalize the costs of maintaining one of their instruments in Canada full time. They made Glenn one of those offers that cannot be refused, and he responded by buying piano 318 from them, thus making it a naturalized Canadian citizen.

Sometime in 1971, it was felt in Columbia Masterworks that Glenn should record some popular concerto works. After all, it had now been several years since the *Emperor,* and although some Bach concertos intervened, the record company longed for the kind of sales that a disc of some juicy large-orchestra concertos would provide. Gould was amenable, and it was decided to record the Grieg Concerto because of its popularity (not to mention Glenn's predilection for that composer, stemming partly from the fact that a distant family relationship could be traced) and the Beethoven Second Concerto because it was the only one of the five that Glenn had not recorded in stereo.

The orchestra chosen was the Cleveland, partially because of its position as one of Columbia's exclusively contracted ensembles and partially because of Glenn's fond memories of its quality—dating from the pre-1964 days when he played there. The conductor was to be Karel Ančerl, then the music director of the Toronto Symphony, with whom Glenn had worked previously. Not too long after the basic plans and contracts were formalized, Ančerl was coincidentally going to be engaged for some concerts with the Cleveland Orchestra. The scheduling was arranged in such a way that the recording could be made without Glenn's actually having to perform the pieces in concert—which, of course, he would have been unwilling to do.

All the plans were finalized, including the arrangements for Columbia Records' portable recording equipment to be shipped to Cleveland. At the appropriate time just previous to the session dates, Glenn had trusty old 318 packed up and shipped to Severance Hall in Cleveland. It arrived safely, and all that remained was for the personnel involved to make the trip. Alas, at practically the last moment, Gould called me with the sad story that he had contracted the flu or some other illness that would necessitate canceling the recording. Naturally, we wondered whether we were hearing the truth or not. But then, what difference would it make? If Glenn didn't want to go to Cleveland, certainly we couldn't force him. We simply had to accept his excuse and set about picking up the pieces.

Our first order of business was the orchestra. The rules of the musician's union that govern recording sessions state that once an orchestra has been booked for a recording, no cancellation is possible within seven days of the event. This meant that Masterworks was going to receive a large bill for the cost of the musicians whether or not we recorded.

The only exception to the regulation involves "acts of God" and requires special rulings from the Federation itself. We at Columbia Records certainly felt that Gould's sudden indisposition could qualify as sufficient reason to approach the union for a dispensation. This we did, and the final ruling was that if we promised to reschedule the sessions (with the same orchestra), they would consider it merely as a postponement and not penalize us for calling off the dates on short notice. Naturally, we were in agreement since we wanted to have these recordings and would reschedule them as soon as the health and timetables of the principal forces involved would allow. Our relief was short-lived, however.

Because of Ančerl's schedule and the schedule of the Cleveland Orchestra, it was not possible to rebook immediately. It looked as if a delay of several months was going to ensue.* Because of this, Gould decided that it would be advisable to have the piano shipped back to Toronto so we could continue on with our various solo projects. He arranged the shipment and I waited for news of his improving health so we could plan our next Toronto sessions. What I did hear next was not quite what I expected.

I believe it was Verne Edquist who first brought us the news. He had been at the Steinway loading dock in Toronto for some other reason and had a question to ask of whoever was in charge at the time. Verne was having a bit of trouble getting someone's attention; everyone there seemed very busy and highly distracted. Finally he virtually had to grab a passerby by the arm and ask his question. The reply was very brusque: "I'm sorry. I can't be

---

*In fact, the two concertos never got recorded. One delay after another continually postponed our rescheduling. Then, Ančerl's death caused the project to become even more remote. However, the partial motivation for choosing Grieg (Gould's distant familial relationship) eventually was satisfied when Glenn recorded the Norwegian composer's piano sonata. Once again, the liner notes were written by Glenn, and they provided an opportunity to tell the Grieg-Gould story.

bothered about that right now. We've just had an accident. Someone's dropped a full-sized grand." The first official word came from the people at Eaton's. "Er . . . excuse me, Mr. Gould, but we think you should come over to the auditorium and look at your piano. It seems that the packing case has sustained a bit of damage as a result of the recent trip."

It didn't take long for Glenn to appear at the top floor of Eaton's to inspect the situation. While he watched nervously, they uncrated the piano. Little by little it became clear that the packing case was not the only thing that was damaged. Piano 318 had suffered severe injury, probably from having been dropped. Of course, the movers knew nothing of this, the people at Severance Hall swore that it left Cleveland in good condition, and, when questioned further, no one at Steinway in Toronto would verify the story that Verne had heard. We all suspected that 318 was dropped just as it was being received at Steinway, but none of us ever discovered what had really happened.

Subsequently, a careful inspection of the piano revealed that it would, indeed, be possible to repair the extensive damage, but this would take time. Reluctantly Glenn had to come to recognize that he was going to be without his favorite piano for the duration of the repairs. What's the old cliché? "Necessity is the mother of invention." Thus was it also with our next recording project.

For some time, Gould had wanted to tape the Handel Suites for Harpsichord. While other works for that instrument had happily poured from piano 318 in past years, this just might be a good time to try some recording on a real harpsichord. One of the major problems that Gould had experienced in the past when attempting to dabble at the harpsichord was the width—and therefore the spacing—of the keys. Most harpsichords had keys that were just a tiny bit narrower than piano keys, and this tended to throw him off as he played. Then, one day, he discovered a large instrument whose key spacing was identical to the piano. He made arrangements for its use, and soon we were back at work recording the first four Handel suites. Glenn loved the sound of this instrument—not a surprising fact when one considers that a large component of his piano-playing style with Baroque literature simulated the sharply etched sound of the harpsichord.

As the sessions progressed, his enthusiasm increased, and one day he reported that he might consider finishing the *Art of the Fugue* on the harpsichord. Gould had recorded volume 1 of Bach's treatise many years earlier on an organ located in a small church in Toronto. Glenn had always intended to complete the project some day, but a serious crimp in his plans occurred when both the church and the organ were destroyed in a fire. When he heard of the tragedy, E. Power Biggs generously offered Gould the use of his organ in Cambridge, Massachusetts. Glenn declined the kind offer, mostly due to the fact that he felt that the sound of Biggs's instrument (readily available for anyone to hear on several recordings of Bach) as well as the acoustic properties of the Busch-Reisinger Museum would not match the original Toronto recording satisfactorily. The basic sound of volume 1 was marked by a closeup, unreverberant image of the organ that, almost by definition, was the antithesis of the usual organ/church combination sought after by builders of "the King of Instruments." Naturally Gould would find it hard to duplicate in the conventional world. Now, however, the textures he was achieving on this harpsichord were so satisfying to him that he began to consider resurrecting the *Art of the Fugue* project and finally producing volume 2. It never happened. His last thoughts on the subject were to abandon the harpsichord idea and start from scratch; recording *both* volumes on the piano. That never happened either.

It has always amused me that upon the release of the Handel record, critics and musicologists had a field day, attempting to draw deep meaning from the fact that after so many years recording on the piano, Gould suddenly switched to the harpsichord. Gleefully they would delve into the psychological ramifications of the change and in every possible way strain to unearth some hidden meaning. Regardless of how hard they tried, the real explanation remained the same: Someone dropped his piano.

Even after the Handel project was concluded, the repairs on 318 were not yet completed and some other piano still needed to be found. Eventually a substitute instrument was located and measures were taken to adjust its mechanism to approximate the qualities of 318. A small amount of electronic equalization was added to the finished tapes to enhance the match. A few albums were actually recorded this way and then, one day, Steinway announced that 318 was ready to return to active duty.

It was with some trepidation that Gould sat down to play the repaired instrument. One thing was immediately apparent: The tone quality that he so treasured was still there. However, the mechanism did not respond exactly as he remembered. This problem sent us off on an odyssey that, I believe, never really ended. He would use 318 for a while, have some adjustments made, pronounce that this was definitely *it,* play some more, find another tiny disturbance, have it adjusted again . . . and so on. Technicians were flown up from New York to make these regulations during the weeks between our sessions. Throughout this period, we continued to use 318 for recording because (1) it still had the quality of sound Gould liked, and (2) the problems it evidenced were subtle and could not be heard in the final taping—they merely made it a bit more difficult for Glenn to achieve the performance he desired. Certainly he was willing to put in the extra effort in order to retain the tonal distinctiveness of 318 on his records.

Somewhere within the last three years of his life, he gave up on 318 altogether and began playing a Yamaha piano. I can only assume he believed that it provided him with an appropriate combination of tactile and acoustical suitability. The switch does seem to indicate, however, that 318 had never quite gotten back into its original mechanical shape. So it joined a growing list of abandoned old friends and colleagues.

6

───

As his creative activities for the Canadian Broadcasting Company (CBC) increased in number and complexity, the amount of recording equipment that Glenn personally owned began to expand. After the initial large purchase, the only significant addition, which I prompted on behalf of the Columbia Records recording project, was the capability for recording on four tracks. In each of the records that involved a musical collaborator—the Bach Violin and Gamba Sonatas, the Hindemith *Marienleben* and brass sonatas—it was desirable to use four-track recording equipment so that the piano and other instrument, or voice, could be kept on separate pairs of tracks and carefully mixed after the sessions. At first, when this kind of collaborative project presented itself, Glenn rented a four-track recorder from a local merchant in Toronto.

When it began to look as if we were all contemplating more sessions of this type, I suggested to him that we might save some rental expense (in the long run) if he were to make the rather nominal investment in the additional parts required to convert one of his own machines to a four-track format. Besides the expense, the major drawback in working with rental equipment is the variability of its condition when it arrives on the job. There is simply no way of telling who used it last and, more important, whether the machine was abused or incorrectly adjusted in any way. By having our own, we could secure for ourselves a more consistent level of reliability.

This was not an unrealistic scheme because the basic parts of an Ampex 440 recorder are identical regardless of the number of tracks—there are just different allotments of them. Therefore, as Glenn owned two two-track machines, he had nearly all the building blocks from which to construct one four-track machine.

Besides certain cabling changes, the only thing that could not be "cannibalized" from his existing two recorders was the four-track head assembly itself. So, with its purchase, I was able rather quickly to convert his setup to four-track capability when needed. In addition, he purchased another small recording console that was necessary for the additional mikes and tracks. He never bought any more microphones as they were quite expensive and could be rented at very reasonable rates in Toronto any time we needed them. It was much safer to rent microphones than tape machines for two important reasons: (1) there are many times the number of adjustments (for potential abuse) contained on a tape machine as compared with a microphone, and (2) the ease of picking up the phone and saying: "This mike is bad, please send over another one" forms a sharp contrast to the difficulty of trying to locate, have delivered (in a truck), and set up an alternate tape recorder.

In fact, the above set of equipment was all that we ever required for conventional CBS recordings. But for his CBC documentary projects, Glenn soon found that eight-track capability was desirable. I don't believe that he ever recorded on all eight at the same time, but he would build his elaborate sonic montages by assembling his final texture little by little on successive tracks that would all play back at the same time. Toward this end, he purchased a Studer eight-track recorder, a medium-size Tascam console, and a Dolby M-16 noise reduction system. These last three acquisitions probably cost as much or more than everything he already owned.

The Dolby units required some customization to make them compatible with his other equipment, so I described for him what he needed to have done, and he made the arrangements. Perhaps it has become clear by now that Gould did not hesitate to spend money if it was channeled into a productive direction. However, when he asked my advice on electronic purchases, I always felt that I had a responsibility to see that he got what he wanted in as economical a fashion as possible. When he reported back with an estimate he had been given for the Dolby modifications, it seemed apparent to me that he was being overcharged. In a phone call I talked at some length about what the alterations involved and why the price was way out of proportion to the actual worth of the job. He patiently waited until I was all done and then told me that he found my concern for his finances "rather touching," but he had no intention of getting additional estimates and would happily pay the price he was quoted.

Such a loose concern about money did not carry over into other aspects of his life. It causes me a bit of discomfort to describe what I next wish to illustrate because it makes it sound as if a record producer expects some sort of remuneration other than his yearly salary. That, of course, is not so, but I had observed for many years that when a producer and an artist have shared a long and productive association, the musician has, on occasion, been moved to provide a token of his appreciation by proffering a gift at Christmastime. Very often a producer must spend incredibly long hours in the preparation of a record. Sometimes a large amount of splicing is necessary to compensate in some way for the artist having had a "bad day" at the time of the recording session. Although it can be argued that this is all part of the job, it certainly is a welcome gesture if the artist makes some expression of his appreciation. Back in my early days with Columbia Records, Vladimir Horowitz presented me with a beautiful cigarette lighter—and I wasn't even his producer, I merely served as editor on a few albums. When my wife and I purchased our house, we were surprised and touched by the unexpected arrival of two lovely silver candlesticks presented to us as a housewarming gift by the Trio of Eugene Istomin, Isaac Stern, and Leonard Rose. Perhaps the most touching of all came after the death of E. Power Biggs when I learned that his personal papers expressed his desire to thank me for our years of work together. I watched as Tom Frost regularly accepted substantial gifts from Eugene Ormandy in view of their long association. In recent years I was happy to be included in the list of New York Philharmonic personnel who received a thoughtful yearly present from Zubin Mehta. One of the most delightful and unique of such appreciative gifts was a year's "subscription" to weekly pizza (my only real vice) given to me as a birthday present by Murray Perahia.

In contrast, Glenn never saw any reason to celebrate the holiday season, and the most I ever received from him at this time of year was a Christmas card—signed by his secretary (maybe that had something to do with lucky checks). He was just one of those people who couldn't say "thank you." If I did some little extra chore for him, he would express his delight at the favorable outcome ("Oh, you made it work! That's terrific! I'm really pleased!"), but the two additional words that would have made all the difference were missing.

On one occasion we actually used his newly purchased eight-track equipment on a Columbia project, the recording of Sibelius's piano music. The genesis of this idea actually began years earlier in New York when we were discussing the upcoming recording of Scriabin's Sonata no. 5. Glenn had already recorded the Third Sonata and was thinking very seriously of proceeding with all the others in order to make an integral set. By pure coincidence, in the midst of our discussions, both Hilde Somer and Ruth Laredo independently burst forth on the market with complete sets. At first, Glenn indicated that this would not dissuade him from completing his own package, but it soon became clear that his enthusiasm for the idea dwindled, and we stopped with only two works recorded.

But the recording of the Fifth Sonata (finally released in 1986) represented something more interesting than the simple continuation of the Scriabin series. Glenn wanted to try an experiment, and I could think of no reason not to go along with the idea. For a long time he had been fascinated by the question of acoustical perspective in the recording of a piece of music, and he wanted to pursue his interest further. Although it gets a little ahead of the story, a concise explanation of his thoughts was contained in a few paragraphs I wrote for the liner notes of the Sibelius album, which serve equally well to express the motivation for the Scriabin recording, thereby making them suitable to reproduce here.

In addition to receiving a rare and revealing look into a little-known corner of Sibelius' *oeuvre,* the listener to this recording will be able to participate in another unusual experience. For want of a better term, let's call it "acoustic orchestration."

Ever since the very first recording of a solo piano, there have been a wide variety of concepts of exactly how the instrument should sound on discs. Should it be projected in a tight, chamber-music-like intimacy?—or across the reverberant span of the concert hall?—or something in between? Record producers have each solved this problem in their own way. However, no matter what solution the combined taste of the artist and producer has yielded, one factor seems to have equal meaning for all of them; the acoustic ambiance must be "right" for the music. Debussy seems to require a more reverberant surrounding than Bach. Rachmaninoff should be bathed in more "grandeur" than Scarlatti.

However, no cognizance ever seems to have been paid to the variations of mood and texture which exist within an individual composition. Why should the staccato articulation of an opening theme be wedded to the larger sense of space required by the lyrical second subject?

Long intrigued by this subject, Glenn Gould offers here a bold and fascinating statement on the appropriateness of space to music. The four works of Sibelius contained in this album were recorded on multi-track tape in a simultaneous variety of perspectives. Microphones were placed in several "ranks" throughout the studio—some only a few inches from the piano, others at a distance of many yards. In the final preparation of the master tape, a mixing plan was devised that favors the image of the instrument most appropriate to the music of the moment. Great care was exercised in planning this "orchestration," which not only varies with the mood engendered by Sibelius' score, but which also serves to underline the inherent structure of the composition.

So, we ask you to put aside any prejudices growing out of traditional approaches and enjoy the extra aesthetic dimension contained in this recording—a mental process not unfamiliar to Glenn Gould's enlightened audience.*

—ANDREW KAZDIN

* In *Glenn Gould: Music & Mind*, Geoffrey Payzant states (p. 139): "CBS Records released in 1977 a disc by Gould of piano pieces by Jan Sibelius. This release is particularly momentous as the first by any performer of classical music in which the mixing process is described in some detail and acknowledged as itself a contributory art. The techniques described in the liner notes are those of the Gould contrapun-

The Scriabin Sonata no. 5 was recorded at Columbia Records' 30th Street studio on eight-track tape and existed in four different, but simultaneously recorded, perspectives. As a kind of "safety valve," the second of these was the pickup of Glenn's piano, which had become standard over the years. In addition, there was a very close pair of mikes, then a distant pair, and finally a *very* distant pickup. The main reason the record was never released in Gould's lifetime stemmed from the fact that the Scriabin project stopped and no logical coupling of works to complete the album ever presented itself. As far as I know, Gould never even inspected the tapes to draw up an editing plan.

After his death, CBS Masterworks diligently searched for any unknown recordings by Gould. It was only a matter of time (four years, to be exact) before they would stumble over the Scriabin Sonata no. 5. In late 1986 CBS contacted me to prepare the piece for release in one of the many anthologies that they were issuing as a kind of extended memorial. This was a welcome but unusual assignment for me because it was the first time that I undertook to choose the takes for a Glenn Gould recording; GG had always reserved that task for himself. A strange kind of Pavlovian reaction set in, and it was clear to me that some little corner of my brain was nervous because I was, in a sense, acting as "the sorcerer's apprentice." When it was time to mix, I simply used the conventional perspective contained in the eight-track tape. No one but

---

tal radio documentaries; Gould has in fact been gradually introducing them into his piano recordings for some time, but this is the first in which they are identified and featured."

Payzant seriously misses the point here, believing (as he seems to) that the momentous feature of the album is the revelation of the techniques rather than the employment of them. We had never before moved in this direction at all, and the last part of his statement is simply nonsense. This flawed accounting of the facts is the inevitable result of writing a biography in a vacuum.

Gould himself could invent an "acoustically orchestrated" scenario such as we had used on Sibelius, years before.

When the idea of recording some piano music of Sibelius was approved by Masterworks, Glenn felt that this might be the perfect opportunity to try once again the multiple-perspective idea; but this time, for a whole album that really would be released. By then we had been working in Toronto for some time and Glenn had just purchased the eight-track equipment that he needed for his CBC activities. His collection of audio equipment had now grown to the point that he needed to rent special office space to store it. At first, it was in a building in downtown Toronto, but eventually he took space in a hotel called The Inn on the Park (a fair distance removed from the center of the city). Not merely a storage area, this location functioned as an editing and mixing facility that Gould used for his CBC projects. He would "borrow" a CBC engineer to run the equipment, but he was free from the red tape of scheduling studio time at the CBC building. The timing was perfect. It worked out conveniently to use his new acquisitions to record Sibelius, and they were all moved into Eaton's for the project. An additional six microphones were rented, as well as a like number of boom stands.

When it came time to do the editing, Frank Dean Dennowitz had to borrow an eight-track playback machine in New York. After that, the edited tape was temporarily brought in to Columbia Records' studios where an identical eight-track copy was made. I would have preferred to make the dub without Columbia's involvement, but to do so would have required two eight-track tape machines, and I considered myself lucky that I was able to scare up one. In any case, this copy enabled me to bring Glenn the finished performance so that he could plan his mixing strategy in advance of actually executing it. How I was able to carry the tape into Canada past their customs officials and then out again—past U.S. Customs officials—is a mystery to me now, and probably stands as a monument to some kind of smooth talking at the time—and a lot of luck.

The first time we recorded in Canada, I was unprepared for the reception I received at the airport when I tried to board my return flight carrying eight reels of recording tape. The carriers from Toronto to New York mainly landed at La Guardia airport. This terminal is not an International Airport and does not contain any facility for Customs or Immigration screening. Therefore, these two processes are conducted at the Toronto end of the trip. It's as if stepping aboard the plane puts the passenger on American soil. When the U.S. Customs official asked me what I was carrying, I indicated the tapes, but did not have the experience to guide him to the correct tariff regulation in his sizable manual. Although one would expect that the officer himself should know where to find the rules that determine the duty he is going to charge the passenger, it did not prove to be so that day, fifteen minutes before my flight was going to depart. The possibilities of tariff ran the gamut from something nominal to an amount that exceeded the original cost of the tapes by a considerable factor.

When it was clear that we could not come to an agreement, the customs man made my trip even more pleasurable by "bonding" the tapes to New York. This meant that they were taken from me before I boarded the plane and needed to be reclaimed at La Guardia, where, after a long wait, I endured, once again, a search of the same manual. Eventually, the correct ruling was located and I discovered that it specified that the duty charge was one cent per *square foot* of the recording tape being transported. Figuring the surface area of a piece of tape one-quarter inch wide and one-half mile long proved to be a rather cumbersome calculation for the average customs officer. Finally, I was told that I owed the U.S. government the princely sum of fifty-two cents per reel: a grand total of four dollars and sixteen cents.

I was determined that this long goose chase was not going to be repeated on future trips, so I noted down all the appropriate information. On subsequent recording ventures north of the border, I would respond to the customs officer by producing the regulation number, the number of square feet I was carrying and the final figure I owed. In general, this approach was effective for the next eight years, but every once in a while, I would encounter a customs officer who was positive that he was going to solve the next *French Connection* caper and would put me through the wringer, asking me to prove, in one case, that these reels were not recorded with a video signal—a high-profit item for U.S. Customs. When I had to transport the eight-track tape for the Sibelius project, I chose to avoid the confrontation.

After Glenn had done all his planning, using the copy tape, we scheduled a time to do the mixing. This had to be done in Toronto because Glenn had to supervise it himself; no one else could possibly have second-guessed a scheme as outrageous as that. So, Frank Dean Dennowitz acted as his engineer, and we worked for two days (a long time to mix a solo piano album) committing his complex choreographic scenario of varying perspectives to a final master tape.

Although Gould called from time to time telling me what a smashing success the "acoustic orchestration" was—he was playing his own copy of the master tape for everyone he could get his hands on—the record itself did not garner particularly good reviews. Musically, everything was status quo; that is, some loved it, some hated it. But the experimental aspect of the album threw certain critics off. Perhaps the most outraged of the reviewers suggested that this recording was either a joke on Kazdin by Gould, or a joke on Gould by Kazdin, or a joke on everyone else by Kazdin and Gould. Nevertheless, it was a bold and unusual experiment, and I am glad we tried it.

The enthusiasm of Glenn's private audiences for the Sibelius, prior to its release, can easily be discounted by remembering that it would take a particularly strong-willed and foolhardy person to withstand one of Glenn's playback performances without succumbing to his point of view. It is highly unlikely that anyone could sit through an hour of watching him conduct the music—underscoring every acoustical nuance with a well-rehearsed dramatic gesture and knowing smile—and then answer his final question: "Well, what do you think? Isn't it terrific?" with anything other than the affirmative. Gould would then come away from the experience carefully carving another notch on his statistical gun.

The Sibelius project was thought up by Glenn alone, but it is not uncommon for the record producer to suggest to his artist repertoire worthy of taping. With Gould, this rarely happened because he knew very well what he wanted to record, and everyone at Columbia Records was keenly aware that he could never be forced to perform something that he was not committed to. However, I remember with some pride that I was actually responsible for suggesting a project that finally came to fruition.

The two-record set of the Hindemith brass sonatas came about as the result of the logical idea that two of the artists with whom I worked might collaborate on a common endeavor. Prior to that time, I had produced three albums with the Philadelphia Brass Ensemble and was pondering what their next project might be. In addition, I was aware that Gould had always shown interest in the music of Paul Hindemith. He had already recorded the three piano sonatas and was contemplating *Das Marienleben*. Therefore, I felt confident in suggesting that an interesting undertaking might consist of bringing the members of the Brass Ensemble to Toronto—one at a time—and recording the four sonatas Hindemith had written for trumpet, horn, trombone, and tuba. Each of these works contained a piano part that, on occasion, demanded a pianist of no less than Gould's virtuosity. Happily, Glenn was receptive to the idea and soon obtained scores of the works so he could study them and make a definite decision.

The players of the Philadelphia Brass Ensemble were informed of our tentative plans, and they were enthusiastic about the project. I felt it was a unique opportunity for the group as it was a chance for each man to display his instrument and talents in a solo capacity, and yet all would contribute to the same project—preserving the spirit of the "ensemble." Finally, all the necessary agreements and approvals were obtained and we considered the recording definitely "on." It only remained for us to find mutually convenient times for the brass players to come to Toronto.

The first sonata to be recorded was the one for trumpet and we scheduled sessions on January 5 and 6, 1975, for Gilbert Johnson to join us. The events of January 5 did not exactly get us off to a great start. Unknown to us, when Gil's plane arrived at the Toronto airport and he started to pass through Customs and Immigration, the trumpet case he was carrying prompted questions about why he was visiting Ontario. When he innocently answered that he was going to record with Glenn Gould, he touched off a tricky situation having to do with foreigners working in Canada. The next thing he knew, he was taken to a private room where he was virtually held prisoner until some verification was obtained that he really was in the employ of CBS in the United States and would be paid by them. One of the things that all internationally traveling musicians know is that this sort of thing comes up frequently, and they should arm themselves with a copy of their employment contract showing exactly who is paying them. Well, as Gil was a member of the Philadelphia Orchestra and almost never traveled outside the United States as a soloist, he did not know all this and, unfortunately, did not have his contract with him. As he could not figure out how to reach either Glenn or me in Eaton's Auditorium on a Sunday afternoon, his anxiety increased as the hour of the first session approached and his temper flared at the Toronto Immigration officials. This didn't help. After being detained for hours, he somehow was able to persuade his captors to try to reach us. Eventually we (who were, by now, a bit upset ourselves at the disappearance of our solo trumpeter) received a call from the airport. I put on my most official-sounding voice and assured the person on the line that I worked for Columbia Records in New York and that indeed Mr. Johnson was being employed by us. This seemed to work, because within another hour or so, a still-fuming Gil Johnson arrived at Eaton's. Between that late-night session and another the next evening, he turned in a beautiful performance of the Hindemith Trumpet Sonata and the project was under way.

Of course, when the rest of the Philadelphia Brass Ensemble heard Gil's tale of intrigue and imprisonment, they each made it a point to bring their contracts with them as they came north, and we had no more recurrences of the immigration situation. In July Mason Jones joined us for the horn sonata, and in September Abe Torchinsky came up to record the tuba sonata. By this time it was becoming obvious that the pieces were timing out just a little longer than we first guessed, and the prospect of fitting all four sonatas on one record was dwindling. Then we discovered that Hindemith had actually written a *fifth* sonata—for alto horn. A quick calculation revealed that if we recorded this piece as well, we would then have the makings of a comfortable two-record set.

In fact, this is indeed what happened. Mason Jones was contacted once more and agreed to perform the additional piece for us. Even though there existed an alternate version of this sonata using the conventional French horn as the solo instrument, Mason chose to play it on the treacherous alto horn itself. Being chiefly employed in military bands, the alto horn is not in popular orchestral usage, and the task of actually locating an instrument that would maintain good tuning throughout its range was no small feat.

The sonata, which we recorded in February 1976, contained one other interesting feature: The fourth movement was preceded by a spoken dialogue that Hindemith wanted recited by the hornist and the pianist. With this short verbal interchange, Mason Jones made his debut on records as a narrator as well as a virtuoso alto horn player. Later in the same month, Henry Charles Smith brought his trombone to Toronto and we finished the set—more than a year after Gil Johnson's first encounter with Canadian bureaucracy.

Shortly after its release, the recording was nominated for a Grammy award as Best Chamber Music Performance of 1976 and won the Record World "Classic Critic's Citation" for the best recording by a brass or woodwind artist. No award was given that year for Outstanding Endurance Shown by a Trumpet Player Held Prisoner in a Foreign Land.

The days of recording in Eaton's Auditorium were, unfortunately, numbered; we were informed in late 1976 that the owners were considering closing the building. Perhaps it was going to be sold, perhaps destroyed. If sold, we wondered, would the auditorium remain intact? There was talk of turning the top floor of the building into office space. We heard a variety of rumors concerning the fate of the room. One would think that someone of Gould's stature (especially in Toronto) would have commanded enough respect of the Eaton's executives to be treated with honesty, but although his contacts were basically polite, it became increasingly apparent that their story changed every five minutes. I sensed that we were never getting an accurate picture. Nonetheless, we knew we would continue to record there until we were definitely told to vacate.

One thing was clear: Eaton's was constructing a multimillion-dollar shopping center just a few blocks down Yonge Street from the present building. It seemed unlikely that they were going to maintain both locations, and so we could probably believe that part of the story. But what would actually become of the auditorium was really undiscoverable. Eventually we were told that in only a certain number of months we would be barred from the building.

Having no idea what the practical consequences of our impending exile was going to have on our recording schedule, we decided to prepare for the worst. This presupposed not only that we would be without Eaton's, but that we would not be able to find another location quickly. So, a kind of crash program was instituted to record as much as possible during the last months of our tenure in the auditorium. This would enable us to continue a more or less unbroken stream of releases (which was really the important issue), and the record-buying public would have no idea we were in trouble. With any luck, some substitute location would be found before our hoard of tapes was exhausted.

My datebook shows that we maintained an intense schedule of sessions in January, February, and March 1977—the last of these being March 29. Then I note a pair of sessions on September 1 and 2, and then nothing. There was no recording for the entire year of 1978—Eaton's had finally closed its doors to us. Although it was obvious that we had better start making plans for another location, there was always a flickering hope that the building would reopen (in some other incarnation) and as long as the auditorium was not destroyed, we might be able to return.

During this period, we continued looking for an alternative site. On April 23 and 24, 1979, we recorded a group of short pieces by Richard Strauss in St. Lawrence Hall. Located within metropolitan Toronto, this building provided us with a kind of ornate ballroom, which was serviceable but was plagued by external noises. We had to set up our control room area in a wide lobby, and working out there was not without problems. The Strauss pieces were not released during Gould's lifetime, but this is not to say that he deemed them unusable. In any case, we knew that we had not yet found a new home.

Then the good news came. Although a certain amount of gutting had already taken place in Eaton's Auditorium, we were informed that the owners were in a kind of holding pattern and if we thought we could still make a usable recording in the place, we were welcome to try. So, in the late spring of 1979, we returned to the old auditorium.

I will not soon forget my first impression upon being led into the hall for the first time in over twenty months. Basically, it looked as if a bomb had hit the place. Walls were missing, doors were boarded up. There were no lights. There was no heat. Our favorite "Green Room" no longer existed. Thick layers of dust covered everything— mostly due to the destruction of so much plaster. Luckily, the freight elevator still functioned so the piano could be brought in. We were given a little closetlike room to set up our equipment. Rather than being in the backstage area, this room was located at the rear of the auditorium, out where the lobby used to be; perhaps it had once been connected to the box office. As we were so far away from the piano, we had to devise extensions to our microphone cables; our original setup was much closer together and our main trunk lines were designed with that distance in mind. A little light bulb hung on a loose wire in this room, and it was necessary for us to import desk and floor lamps in order to see what we were doing. Similarly, at the piano, a solo improvised light was rigged up so that Glenn could consult the music if necessary.

Ray Roberts informed me of the giant cleanup operation that had already taken place even before I saw this shambles. From time to time, as we talked, he sprayed air freshener into all corners of our control closet. When I questioned him about it, he told me that it was quite necessary as they had discovered, in the midst of straightening out the place, that an adjacent cubbyhole had come equipped with samples of human excrement. I thanked him for his consideration.

The most bizarre aspect of this London-in-the-midst-of-World-War-II movie set didn't occur until the autumn months of 1979. I see by my notes that we recorded in this disaster area for a total of fourteen days, grouped into six trips, and taking place once a month through October 11, 1979. As the weather got colder, the lack of heat in the building became a real liability, for late nights in Canada could be chilly. Never willing to succumb to a challenge, and, I'm sure, secretly enjoying the grotesque nature of the experience, Glenn and Ray arranged for four large space heaters to be brought into the hall when we used it. These devices, somewhat resembling jet engines, were placed in the aisles of the auditorium and were powered by tanks of gas. They emitted a furnacelike roar and could be turned on only when we were not actually taping. So the room would be brought up to a temperature that would sustain human life, and then the heaters would be turned off so that music could be recorded. From time to time throughout the evening, the hall was given a kind of "booster shot" of heated air. Glenn, of course, performed at the piano wearing an overcoat and scarf—no gloves. Verne Edquist, loyal as ever, uttered a few more "By gollys" than usual, kept the instrument in tune under these very difficult circumstances, and continued to supply us with sustenance from the outside world—more valuable than ever since there was no running water in the building (did I forget to mention that?). In retrospect, my mind makes the logical leap from the question of drinking water to the more serious lack of toilet facilities. The human brain is merciful in what it will allow us to remember, and I have effectively blocked that whole issue. I have vague memories of having to take the elevator down to the ground floor and then walking down a flight of stairs where, because of a still-functioning entry to the

Toronto subway system, a public washroom was maintained.

It was not until six years after his death that I made a most awesome discovery. I learned that among Gould's personal effects a large number of notepads were unearthed. Written in his own hand, these pads contained a wide variety of texts. Sketches for repertoire investigation, shopping lists, reports of his eating activities, and practically all other manner of daily reminders made up the contents. Most interesting, however, was the fact that among these pads there existed a smaller "subset" that chronicled one particular subject: Either real or imagined, Glenn had developed some physical problem with his hands. He describes his growing concern that he was losing control of his fingers. Of course, these words have a different meaning for a pianist than they do for the rest of us. In Gould's profession, "losing control" could mean the inability to play difficult technical passages with the same fluency as he was used to—and as the public had come to expect from his performances. He wryly muses that probably no one else could tell he was experiencing these problems. Nonetheless, his fear was intense. He writes about numbness in his arms and fingers. He attempts to chalk off the condition to the depression he felt at the recent passing of his mother. He describes his activities doing private "test" recordings for the purpose of judging the severity of this new affliction. And most alarmingly, he relates that he took a year off from his work for CBS Masterworks.

I must hurry to explain what a shock all of the above was when I learned of it. First, the very existence of the notepads was a surprise. It has been advanced that it is not uncommon for people to use the mechanism of privately writing down their thoughts as a way of gaining some distance from them and thereby viewing them with a measure of objectivity. But this explanation did not fit the Gould I knew. I would have surely believed him to be the person most likely to have the perspective to see his own mental processes in the same kind of all-encompassing snapshot that he was capable of using to analyze a complex musical composition. The suggestion that he needed the crutch of committing his thoughts to paper before he could fully understand them just didn't make sense. Naturally, the other possible explanation—that he was simply preparing notes for an autobiography—could not be overlooked. In any case, the pads were being produced throughout the entire period of our relationship, and I had absolutely no clue they existed.

Much more important than the presence of the pads was the revelation of the hand problem. Need I bother to add that I did not have the slightest suspicion of this fact either. At the point in the chronicle that states it was necessary for him to take a one-year hiatus from our work together, I found myself uncontrollably voicing a response. "Nonsense! He never took a year away from recording! Well, of course there was the year we lost in 1978 because of the unavailability of Eaton's, but that had nothing to do with physical problems. That was because they wouldn't let us in. You see . . ." Then it hit me. Everything I knew of the Eaton situation I had learned from Glenn. I had never attempted to verify any of the facts of the case. I had simply accepted his word, a practice that I now know to be fraught with peril. It all dawned in a cascade of realizations. It was absolutely possible that the Eaton delay was a fiction concocted by Gould to disguise the real reason for the cessation of recording activities. Of course, the auditorium really was being destroyed; I saw that for myself. But that inexplicable delay—the one where I could not learn any firm facts about Eaton's plans for the building; the one where I wondered why they weren't being more communicative with Glenn— *that* delay was probably an invention of Gould's. My curiosity prompted a phone call to Ray Roberts. He felt that the truth lay somewhere in between. There really was a delay caused by Eaton's, but it was not as long as I was told. The situation fell right into Glenn's hands; he simply stretched things a bit until he felt he was again capable of performing up to his personal standards. And so, ten years after the fact, I discovered that I too had been the victim of creative lying. He had orchestrated the whole thing so carefully that I never once suspected that he had entered into (and successfully emerged from) a period of crisis. And, of course, the whole story confirms once more the segments into which he divided his life—and the way he apportioned those segments among his acquaintances.

Throughout all our years working in Toronto, it had become our habit to have lengthy talks after our recording sessions. Even though the Westbury Hotel, where I stayed almost exclusively, was only one block from Eaton's, when we finished recording I would accompany Glenn to his car, help him push aside the piles of magazines and music that were scattered everywhere, get in, and have him give me a lift back to my temporary home. Usually, on the first night of the trip, I was still suffering from the effects of the plane ride—compounded by the session itself—so I was pretty tired and wanted to go to sleep promptly. Even though this could be two or three in the morning, I was always able to get a good night's sleep because my next firm appointment wasn't until six or seven the following evening. Sometimes I could sleep well past noon, so when the next night's session was over, I was still in good, rested condition. After Glenn drove me to the Westbury, it was very common for us to sit in his car in front of the hotel and talk for an hour or more. These talks could cover any subject: things on his mind, things on mine. Much of what I learned about his patterns of thought was gleaned in these early-morning discussions.

In early 1979 we had a long talk on a subject of some importance to me. It had been becoming clear that things at Columbia (now called CBS) Records were shifting in a most unpleasant way for me personally. A succession of

Masterworks Department vice presidents created increasing chaos for the producers. Finally in July 1979 a man named Simon Schmidt was given the entire responsibility for CBS Masterworks worldwide. When Schmidt first assumed the position, it looked as if he might bring a much-needed sense of order to a highly fragmented and disorganized operation. Alas, the job proved a bit too much for him, and after holding it for nine months, he was given a "leave of absence" from which he never returned. In any case, as these regimes overlapped each other and created a disturbing atmosphere totally unlike the one I had once known (not to mention the one in which I wished to continue working), it became increasingly apparent to me that it would not be long before I would find it impossible to continue to work at CBS. It was this issue that occupied a good deal of our current post-session auto talks.

One question dominated in our talks: If I was to leave CBS, could I count on the income derived from a continuing involvement in Glenn's recordings? By this I did not mean the flat fee I had been receiving to use my own studio facilities while editing his tapes. I had been forced to give that up when one of the many Überführers that breezed through the top levels of our department felt that it "looked bad" to have a full-time employee of Masterworks receiving any additional payment, even if it was for work that was above and beyond what he had originally been hired to do, and (illogically) even if it saved his department thousands of dollars.

The income I *was* referring to was of an entirely different sort. A "master purchase" agreement is an arrangement between a record company and performing artist, which essentially puts the responsibility and costs of producing a finished master tape in the hands of the artist. The contract further specifies an inclusive figure representing what the artist will be paid to allow the company to press, distribute, and sell recordings made from these tapes. As Gould's Toronto operation differed from this kind of agreement by only a small amount, I proposed that he consider making the transition complete by becoming his own production organization, which would sell finished master tapes to CBS. The only difference from his old method of operation would be that Gould would pay my fee as an independent producer and then build an appropriate increment onto his charge to Masterworks. I explained that there was no particular hurry in making this decision, but I merely wanted to know whether he was amenable to the notion should I sever my connection with CBS. Gould expressed what I would call "guarded" interest in the proposition and went on to explain that he had been planning his own stratagem as regards CBS Masterworks.

After swearing me to secrecy, he revealed his plan. By this time in our relationship, I had taken the oath of silence so many times that it might have proved wise to have had standard forms printed up. He began by explaining that his master timetable for his own career slated the cessation of recording when he reached fifty years of age. He reasoned that he would have completed all his major projects (the solo music of Bach and the Beethoven sonatas as well as the two missing Bach keyboard concertos) by that time and it would be appropriate to start a new phase in his musical life, perhaps involving conducting. He assured me that, as he was approaching forty-seven when we spoke, he would plan a recording schedule that would fit in all the necessary recordings in the short span of three years. He went on to say that as long as his association with CBS (as a pianist) was going to last only thirty-six more months, he could see no reason to have to "break in" a new producer, and I could expect his cooperation if CBS approved the master purchase arrangement. He probably had no idea that his expression implied that my chief value to him was that I had "learned the ropes." It was a little hurtful to hear these words. Although still uncomfortable from hearing his weak statement of loyalty, I listened as he revealed an even more interesting scheme.

If *Machiavellian* was a term possibly equated to the process of creative lying, it most definitely was applicable here. I don't believe I ever witnessed a creative artist cold-bloodedly give birth to a scheme as mercenary as the one Gould now unfolded for me. It went like this: He would announce to the world in general (and CBS Records in particular) that he would abandon recording at age fifty, and he would negotiate his next contract with Master-works to run out at exactly the right moment. However, after all of the above was accomplished, he would continue to record secretly in Toronto. These tapes would all be processed into finished masters and simply stockpiled. Glenn reasoned that after he had made his announcement to stop recording, the value of his records would increase as they became collector's items. Finally, when a sufficient time had elapsed (five years? ten years?), he would reveal some or all of his hidden catalog and reap the benefits of their newfound value. He had grand visions of selling to the highest bidder. It certainly was an interesting plan, and I could not resist asking whether there would be a place for me in that setup. His answer was much more noncommittal than the response relative to the next three years of CBS projects. I wondered at the time why this was, as he undoubtedly was going to need someone to put these tapes together for him. I dismissed the thought and chalked the evasiveness up to just another one of Gould's security measures, and the conversation ended.

It is interesting to note a parallel situation that was exactly the opposite of the "buried treasure" scheme. In one case, Glenn was trying to amass a vault full of tapes to salt away for the future; in the other, he found himself faced with the problem of not knowing how to "unload" certain recordings that had been made over the years and not released. There was nothing wrong with the latter recordings, they were merely orphans in the CBS Master-works icebox that could not find suitable coupling material. The company had always been unified on one subject:

Let Glenn record anything he wanted. It was not a big risk. Whatever the piece, if Gould found it worth his while and effort, certainly CBS could be proud to have it in the can. So, over the years, an interesting variety of short pieces began to appear in our vaults. There were some sonatas by Domenico Scarlatti, a short work by C. P. E. Bach, a pair of pieces by Scriabin, the remains of the ill-fated *Ophelia Lieder* with Schwarzkopf, the first movement of the aborted attempt at the Liszt transcription of Beethoven's Sixth Symphony, and "So You Want to Write a Fugue."

This last was an interesting case all in itself. It was a piece Glenn had composed himself for vocal quartet and string quartet. The lyrics proffer tongue-in-cheek advice for the novice contrapuntalist while the music displays a solidly constructed baroque fugue. For the recording, an impressive assemblage of musicians (including the Juilliard Quartet) was conducted by Vladimir Golschmann. All this took place in the early 1960s, and it had found only one avenue for distribution—the one for which it had been created. It was pressed on one of those very thin, flexible sheets of plastic that occasionally can be found sandwiched into periodicals. In fact, that is exactly how it was released—within the pages of the magazine *High Fidelity*. Subsequent to this quaint exposure, this charming novelty languished in Columbia's vaults for well over a decade. Certainly Glenn would have been pleased if some method for releasing it to the record-buying public could have been found. So it shared company with the other short pieces cited above. Many times he and I joked about this collection of strange bedfellows and their doomed existence.

Soon after Vladimir Horowitz had made his triumphant return to concert-giving in the early 1970s, Glenn hit on a "very funny" plan that would take the form of a takeoff of the Horowitz situation and, at the same time, clean out these assorted small pieces from Columbia's "icebox." The idea did not meet with any enthusiasm from the leaders of Masterworks, and my files contain a collection of interoffice memos written at the beginning of 1974 that clearly condemn the idea. One of them remarked that Gould wasn't as funny as he thought he was. All of this culminated in a letter to Gould that explained that they had all come to the conclusion that it would not be "dignified" for Columbia Records to release the album. This put an end to the project—for the moment.

It is probably true that ideas don't change, only the executives who are temporarily paid to evaluate them. Glenn merely had to wait for a new opportunity to present itself. The fabled "knock" came in a rather unusual way. In late 1979 he became cognizant of the fact that the following year marked his twenty-fifth anniversary with CBS Masterworks. He confided to me that he was a little bit hurt that no one in the upper echelons of the department seemed to be planning any kind of celebratory gesture. After all, he had been loyal to them for twenty-five years (shunning whatever offers may have come his way from competing companies), which is a notably long period. I felt moved to suggest to my superiors in a tactful way that they were on the verge of making a real blunder if they let this important anniversary pass unheralded. Back in New York, I set about the task of subtly indicating the need for a celebration. Finally my bosses saw the importance of the observance and plans started to be formulated.

Record companies think like record companies, and the obvious form of this gesture would be a special record release. But what repertoire should be collected to offer in this package? Glenn was waiting with the answer. He simply needed to be asked. Once unleashed on the officials of Masterworks, his superlative abilities as a salesman produced a result that embodied the following features:

1. The repertoire was varied and interesting.
2. The scheme disposed of all the detritus gathering dust in the vault.

3. It provided Gould the opportunity to produce another of those multi-character discussions of which he was so fond.

4. It gave him great personal satisfaction to package up all these unreleasable elements and "sell" them back to Masterworks who now became the unwitting accomplice in a real put-on.

In 1980 Columbia Masterworks proudly released the Glenn Gould *Silver Jubilee Album.* I believe that in this process, he secretly had paid them back for turning down the idea six years earlier and for having to be prompted to remember this important anniversary of one of their most prestigious artists.

As the winter of 1979 approached, and the atmosphere within Masterworks more and more resembled that of a berserk police state, I feared that my theoretical talk with Glenn would quite likely flower into practical reality. There seemed little hope for the future at CBS under the present regime, and everyone in the department was trying to formulate some plan of survival. A few people within our group considered quitting, but those of us with long years of employment at CBS saw that voluntary withdrawal would eliminate the possibility of severance pay.

Glenn was continually made aware of the newest developments within the Masterworks Department. He always relished the gossip (and the chance to play Twenty Questions), but constantly made it known that although he never doubted my word for a minute, he was not personally witness to any of the strange behavior rampant in our leadership. This was the period when Eaton's was being resurrected from the ashes and because of our long absence from recording, we were now having sessions every month. Naturally, many hours of talk were devoted to the subject, and Glenn always seemed friendly and supportive to me.

My own personal crisis came to a head in late November when I was scheduled to record the Brahms Fourth Symphony and the Chopin First Piano Concerto with the New York Philharmonic (with Murray Perahia as soloist in the Chopin). Here is not the place to delve into a detailed explanation of exactly what led up to these recording sessions, but suffice it to say that a difference of opinion existed between Simon Schmidt and myself about whether the recordings should be made using the newly introduced digital process. Whereas I did not, and still do not, have any prejudices about digital recording in general, the equipment supplied for my use brought a concomitant handicap along with the advantages of the new technology. I weighed the issues very seriously and finally decided to make the recording in the conventional way, without digital processing. I announced this to the engineers and to the artists when I arrived for the first session. The recording itself went smoothly and we were all pleased with the results.

The day following the last session was a different matter, however. Paul Myers (who had returned to New York as one of the succession of new department heads) asked me how things had gone. I answered in the affirmative. Then, as a kind of double check, he added: "You *did* record in digital?" I simply said, "No." At first he looked as if he hadn't understood me—or maybe he doubted the evidence of his own ears—so he asked again. I explained my position and reconfirmed for him the fact that no digital tapes had been made. His reply was: "Well, if it were up to me, I'd fire you here on the spot!" and he bolted from my office.

It didn't take much imagination to guess what was going to happen when, on Monday, December 3, I was called to a meeting in Schmidt's office. This was the first time we had spoken since the Philharmonic sessions, and he proceeded to explain what a horrendous deed I had committed. He went on to say that my act rendered the tapes of the Brahms and Chopin practically worthless, and I should consider myself lucky that I was not being sued for the cost of the sessions. Finally he explained that he had no choice but to "terminate" me. In Orwellian terms, this could have been a process whereby several thousand volts of electricity were passed through my brain, but in 1979 corporation parlance, it merely meant that I was fired. I waited, breathless, as he described the details of the separation because the really crucial matter had not yet been discussed. Then he said it. Indeed, because of my long years of service, and so on, CBS had decided to give me my severance pay. This amounted to the better part of four months' salary and so was not to be sneezed at. I left his office. I was free!

I was given the rest of that week to clean up my affairs, which placed the end of my employment on Friday, Pearl Harbor Day, 1979. (Parenthetically, I should say that both the Brahms Fourth Symphony and the Chopin First Piano Concerto were released soon after with no discernible ill effects because of my unthinkable act.) In retrospect, I can look back on the episode with a philosophical eye, as the technical issues that had caused me to make my decision in the first place were shortly resolved by the succeeding management, thereby clearing the way for my colleagues to employ digital technology without any compromises.

When I told Glenn—or rather, when he finally guessed the Twenty Questions game of the day—his first reaction was: "Well, congratulations!" I explained that I was being asked to return all his unedited tapes to CBS and had no idea what nature of conversation might ensue on the subject of my continuing work in Toronto.

At the time of my leaving, four artists occupied the bulk of my time at CBS. Besides Glenn, I produced the recordings of the New York Philharmonic, Isaac Stern, and Murray Perahia. There were many conversations in every conceivable direction, and one of the chief issues was whether Masterworks would allow me to continue to work with any of them on a free-lance basis. Schmidt's attitude was negative, but Paul Myers told me that if there was any chance at all, it would be with Glenn, as the circumstances of our operation in Toronto were special, and because there were probably only a handful of records left to go (Paul also knew about Glenn's decision to stop recording at age fifty, but I'm not sure whether he was aware of the "buried treasure" scheme), Schmidt could probably be convinced to let me finish up with Gould rather than rock the boat of artist relations at the last minute. Paul said he would continue to speak with Schmidt about the idea and would let me know. Myers's benevolent attitude seemed in sharp contrast to his earlier one of wanting to fire me on the spot.

Recording sessions had been planned in Toronto for December 26 and 27 (notice Glenn's usual lack of observance of the holiday season), and I had already booked my airplane and hotel reservations. Under normal circumstances, Glenn and I would be in touch once or twice in the week preceding the sessions just to make final checks and confirm what repertoire he had prepared so I could be sure to bring the proper music with me. In this case, I received no call, and as I had not heard from Paul either, I was beginning to get nervous. So, either on Sunday the twenty-third or Monday the twenty-fourth, I tried to telephone Glenn to discover if any plans had been solidified. At first I couldn't reach him, but I persisted. Sometime during the evening I called his studio number and he picked up the phone. He seemed very tense and immediately asked if he could call me back at another time. At that late date I needed the information vitally, so I answered, "No, I have to ask you a question. Do we have sessions on Wednesday and Thursday?" He acted surprised and queried, "Didn't Paul speak to you?" I replied that he hadn't and that I really would like to find out what was going to happen the following week. By then I became aware that someone was with him in his studio, and some sixth sense told me it was a woman. Clearly, he wanted to get off the phone, but I was on the brink of making a plane trip and I had to find out if the sessions were on or off. Glenn must have realized I wasn't going to relent and then said: "Well, as you know, I've been in discussion with Paul about this whole matter. He tells me that Simon Schmidt absolutely refuses to have you continue producing my records. So, Paul tells me that I have only two options: Either I accept another CBS producer, or I produce the records myself. Naturally, I chose the latter." I was a bit stunned and asked, "Does this mean that our association is over?" He answered in a very hurried fashion: "Yes. Now, don't be a stranger. Let's talk from time to time. Maybe I'll see you if I ever get down to New York. Look, I've really got to go. Good-bye." All I could utter were the two syllables "Good-bye . . ."

I never heard from him again. Thus ended our fifteen-year relationship. No regrets, no emotion, no thank yous.

At a convenient moment, I spoke with Paul Myers in order to hear his story. Apparently there was something he was supposed to tell me, but I had gotten through to Glenn before he had had the chance. Paul said that he had made good headway with Schmidt and that it had been virtually agreed upon that I could continue with Gould. Then he had spoken with Glenn, who had said that it was common knowledge how much he had always wanted to produce his own recordings and this would be a good time to start. Paul made it clear that Glenn himself opted to work without me.

Clearly, someone was lying (how creatively, I'll never know). My suspicion was that Paul's story was the true one and Glenn simply could not face up to telling me himself. Of course, there were still several unanswered questions. Why did Glenn suddenly turn on me that way? I could detect no deterioration in our relationship throughout 1979 and, in fact, I remembered the conversation with him earlier that year in which he agreed to investigate an arrangement by which I could continue to work on his records if I ever left CBS. Furthermore, I could think of no reason why he would want to produce his records without me as he always had maintained complete artistic control, and I had long since established my credentials with him as a trustworthy collaborator. My value on his projects could only be thought of as positive—with absolutely no "interfering" influence. All I could think of was that in the last year or so, a personal dislike had developed and Gould, aware of all the utilitarian worth that my contributions to his sessions afforded him, decided to carry on with me, figuring the good outweighed the bad. Of course, his masterful expertise at role playing prevented me from suspecting that anything was festering.

At some point during the following year, I heard from a friend that Bruno Monsaingeon, a television director who occasionally worked with Glenn, had disclosed some remarks that Gould had made about our relationship. Supposedly Bruno had heard Glenn say that I had exerted a bad influence on his piano playing and therefore the association had to be dissolved. This certainly sounded a little fishy to me because of the obvious fact that for fifteen years I had meticulously avoided having *any* influence on Gould's playing. Besides, whatever atmosphere I encouraged at his recording sessions must have been the correct one—there is no other explanation for our uninterrupted association of one and a half decades. History showed quite clearly that Gould was not hesitant about changing record producers if he was unhappy. By pure coincidence, in late 1982 I worked on a television production directed by Monsaingeon and had the opportunity of finding a quiet moment to bring up the subject. Bruno not only denied that he ever said such a thing, but he denied that he and Glenn had even had such a conversation.

CBS Masterworks learned about Glenn's stroke shortly after he was hospitalized, and one of the members of the department with whom I had maintained a warm relationship called me out of courtesy to transmit the news.

It was a surprise, but not a complete surprise. By that I mean that I had known about Gould's high blood pressure for several years and was also aware of his continuing use of sedatives and tranquilizers. Valium and hand-soaking were the components of his pre-session ritual and probably would have preceded his concert performances had he continued to play in public. All of us near him would hear him casually talk from time to time about how he was unable to sleep the night before and how he had to take a Nembutal. Little by little these tales increased in frequency until it seemed clear to us that he was developing a real dependency on this substance. It formed a problem for those who cared for him. Occasionally, someone would try to broach the subject and appeal to his intellect to get him to stop taking this dangerous narcotic, but the attempt would always be gently rebuffed by Gould.

Although this kind of drug abuse does not guarantee early mortality for the user, it certainly acts as a warning. Of course, even with this knowledge, the news of the catastrophe was unexpected. Soon after, the newspapers carried the story. On October 2, *The New York Times* reported the incident with particular attention to the question of residual paralysis of his hands. There was really no clue at this point that he would not survive. Once again, it was Masterworks that told me of his death on October 4, 1982, one week after the initial attack.

To say that Glenn's passing engendered within me a complex chain of profound emotional responses falls short of expressing what I actually felt. We had maintained a close working relationship for over fifteen years, and, in addition, I could not help but feel that we had become friends as well. When I dwell on that aspect of our association, I feel his loss as keenly as anyone would mourn the departure of a friend—not to mention the loss to the musical world. However, this very feeling of closeness caused me to feel great pain and some anger after that terrible phone call in which Glenn abruptly and unexpectedly ended our long association. I would not be telling the truth if I did not admit that fleeting thoughts of retribution crossed my mind. This is not a pleasant emotion to recognize, and its presence disturbed me greatly.

Shortly after Glenn's death, I placed a telephone call to Ray Roberts. This was the first contact we had had since our last recording in Toronto, which had been a three-day affair spanning October 9–11, 1979. We had a long talk in which he explained some of the details of Gould's fatal stroke, discussed the imminent memorial service in Toronto, and tried to answer the one question that had been on my mind for three years: What had gone wrong? I felt that if anybody could tell me, Ray could. But Ray said he really didn't know. In an effort to be helpful, he asked if, perchance, I had ever asked Glenn any questions about any lady friends and went on to say that if I had, then it was very likely the cause of our separation. Well, I hadn't, so that could not have been the reason, although I could not help but wonder whether making a simple inquiry into Glenn's social life was really a crime worthy of such an extreme reaction.

Ray tried to explain that his observations of Gould's behavior in other long-term associations indicated that there really didn't need to be any logical cause for the split. It seems that when he got tired of using people, he simply turned them off. I remember that a portion of my talk with Bruno concerned Glenn's friendship with Yehudi Menuhin. I never heard Gould say anything derogatory about the violinist, but apparently, during my three-year "blackout," a rift had developed between them. More properly, Yehudi had made some joke that Glenn perceived as not being funny, and the pianist immediately decided that this man could no longer be his friend. As I recall, the bad joke had nothing to do with Gould, music, or any other subject common to the two of them. It just touched some sensitive nerve in Glenn—rather like the incident involving *Cosmopolitan* magazine. In light of the foregoing, it is a bit curious to note that when, in 1987, the Glenn Gould Memorial Foundation created "The Glenn Gould Prize," the international jury selected to administer the award included both Bruno Monsaingeon and Yehudi (now *Sir* Yehudi) Menuhin.

It was also during this conversation with Ray Roberts that I was sad to learn of the dismissal of Verne Edquist. Ray told me that seats for the memorial service were very scarce, but if I wanted to fly up to Toronto, he would hold a place for me. I thanked him for his thoughtfulness but indicated that I was experiencing very strong mixed feelings and I really didn't know if I could make the trip. In a kind effort to try to make up my mind for me, Ray said: "Look, why don't you just come?" I said I would think about it. Naturally, I thought long and hard about it.

Even before he had given up concertizing in 1964, Glenn had ceased flying. Before that, he had been performing in cities practically around the globe and had flown in almost every kind of plane that existed at the time. He told me why he had given it up and it was as simple as this: He said he woke up one morning and said to himself, "What are you doing? What are you *doing?*" In that instant of revelation, he decided that it just was not worth the risk, and he never set foot in an airplane again. One night after a recording session, he stated that he was concerned because I flew so much—particularly to Toronto for his benefit. He once again reiterated that he could not have done it if the situation were reversed, and he shook his head in wonder about my frequent air trips in order to work with him. He said, "I just don't see how you do it." Well, I've never been relaxed about flying, but I do it when I must. I thought about all of this after Ray extended the invitation to come to the memorial service. Glenn was right; I had risked my life repeatedly to make his records. I decided that I would risk it no more for him or for his memory. I declined the invitation.

Epilogue

There were two spine-chilling ironies associated with Gould's death. The more macabre of these was the fact that he died nine days after his fiftieth birthday, thereby assuring the truth of his oft-repeated prediction that he would stop recording at that age. The other had to do with the exact cause of death.

He suffered a massive stroke on September 27, 1982, and shortly thereafter fell into a coma. I learned from Ray Roberts that the most important medical priority for a stroke victim is for the doctors to control the swelling of the brain. Apparently the trauma of the incident causes the brain to enlarge, and unless this can be reversed, the pressure within the skull damages the tissues and causes death. For exactly one week after the stroke (actually, I believe Glenn suffered more than one stroke), doctors administered every kind of treatment known to them in an effort to reduce the swelling of his brain. But it would not respond and eventually brought about his demise.

The irony here is overwhelming. His brain—which imbued him with the rare gift of absolute pitch, which held within itself the brilliant and unique musical interpretations that poured forth over his career, which could memorize the most complex scores of Schönberg and Hindemith, which was probably the only single repository of all the pieces of the jigsaw puzzle into which he had fragmented his life—this brain, his greatest asset, is what killed him.

Appendix 1

Slaughterhouse Five

The only time I became involved in a project of Gould's that was not for CBS was when he was contacted in 1971 by the director George Roy Hill to organize the music sound track for the motion picture *Slaughterhouse Five*. I use the word *organize* because that best described Glenn's activities. Hill wanted the background score to be composed completely of the music of Bach, and Glenn's reputation as a performer of this repertoire was so respected and widespread that his name came to mind immediately. Hill was not particular where the music came from (as long as Gould performed it). In fact, several of the selections were simply taken from existing Gould recordings (much to the delight of Columbia Records, which made its own financial arrangement with the movie company) and only a little was recorded especially for the occasion. Besides a short connecting interlude of Glenn's own devising (playing on the harpsichord), only two major pieces were recorded directly for the film.

First, there was an interesting ending (also composed by Gould) that diverted the Bach D Major Concerto from its intended course and guided it into Gould's harpsichord cadenza.

This, in turn, led to the other orchestral selection, the *Branden-burg* Concerto no. 4. Members of the New York Philharmonic were hired to become a nameless studio orchestra to assist Gould here as well as in the keyboard concerto. The solo violin and flute parts were played by Rafael Druian and Julius Baker, respectively, and I acted as audio producer for the sessions.

In retrospect, the fact that Glenn requested that I produce the new recordings for the film probably was motivated chiefly by convenience. The sessions were to take place in Columbia's 30th Street studio, New York musicians were employed, and Gould was traveling to New York especially for the recordings. Under these conditions, it would have been a bit silly to bring in another production team to replace the one that was completely at home in that hall. In addition, as one of his key ideas involved splicing his trick ending onto his already released performance of the D Major Concerto, it made sense to involve me in the new recording as it had to match the old album, which I had produced. It is difficult to be objective in judging this situation, but I find myself discounting this one project and continuing to think of Gould's outside activities as being accomplished specifically without my involvement.

Of course, in the manner of all film sound tracks, when the required number of minutes of the *Brandenburg* had been recorded, we just stopped. This left the excerpt as a kind of "bleeding chunk" that could not be used conveniently in any other context. Later, I will come back to this liability when I discuss the sound-track album that emerged from this endeavor. Peculiarly, this interesting excerpt, never before (or since) touched by Gould, will probably forever remain trapped exclusively in the film.

Besides playing the continuo part for the *Brandenburg*, Glenn interpolated a few bars of organ into the texture. In the film, the music accompanies the procession of the American prisoners through the town of Dresden. When a large cathedral is passed, Gould (in the best Mickey Mouse tradition) highlights the event with the sound of an organ. There was, of course, no organ in the Columbia studio, so it was planned to overdub a real church instrument after the orchestral performance was edited. Unfortunately, Gould had to return to Toronto and could not wait in New York for a church to allow us to record a handful of measures on their organ. It was decided that John Strauss, who was the music editor assigned to the film and who had some experience playing the organ, would overdub the passage in Glenn's absence. Probably Gould would have played the part right from his head, but for Strauss he carefully wrote down what he wanted to hear.

The only problem associated with the organ recording was matching the pitch of the instrument to the pre-recorded orchestra. With a little electronic manipulating, John Strauss became part of the *Brandenburg* Concerto. Gould returned to New York a short time later and supervised the blending of the various effects he had created.

While all of this was going on, another little drama was being played out over the telephone and in the mails. With one of its leading classical artists involved in a major motion picture, Columbia Records management was rubbing its hands together at the prospect of issuing the original sound-track album. The company was soon to discover that Universal Pictures had its own ideas. Much dialogue ensued. It quickly became clear that each company wanted to release the album under its own name and pay the other a small royalty. The situation was complicated by the fact that CBS already owned all the basic Gould performances except the newly recorded material (the latter obviously owned by Universal, as it paid for all the sessions). Each felt that the other needed *it* to round out the whole record, and although Universal owned only a small minority of the music, it believed that it held the trump card in that the words ORIGINAL SOUNDTRACK ALBUM could not be appended to the package without its permission, which would have to be bought and paid for. The struggle continued and finally ended in a draw; that is, neither company would allow the other to use its unique property.

As soon as this stalemate had become clear, we at Masterworks put our heads together and decided that we would release what is known in the trade as a "cover album." This means that one record company will try to cash in on the success of another by getting one of its contracted artists to record the same material included in the competitor's hit album. For example, in popular music, a typical situation might be that Kapp Records issues the Original Cast Album of the Broadway show *The Man of La Mancha,* and then Columbia Records issues an album titled *André Kostelanetz Plays the Hits from "Man of La*

Mancha." It's always an attempt on the part of the second company to capitalize on the drawing power of its "name" artists as a substitute for their weak position as an "also-ran" contender.

In the *Slaughterhouse Five* situation, we had the unique circumstance of the cover album being played by the very same artist who recorded the film! Universal could not stop CBS from reissuing some of its own Gould performances. In fact, this is exactly what happened. We duplicated everything that Gould had used in the film, but had to substitute a Casals performance of the Fourth *Brandenburg* instead of the Gould snippet, which would have been nearly impossible to use even if Universal had given us the rights to release it; don't forget, it had no ending—it just stopped. The crowning touch, if I do say so myself, was the wording I suggested to be put on the cover: "Music from *Slaughterhouse Five*—featuring Glenn Gould's Original Performances Heard in the Film." Nothing could have been more explicit (or truthful), yet it did not violate Universal's prohibition to use the words *Original Soundtrack.* Universal Pictures, of course, could still issue the three or four minutes that it had commissioned especially for the film, but for some reason declined to do this. Gould quietly sat by at the sidelines watching this battle of wits without participating in any way. He could not lose; whoever released the album would have to pay him royalties.

Appendix 2

Discography

Although Gould made a few records for other companies, the vast majority of his recorded output appeared on Columbia Masterworks, eventually to be known as CBS Masterworks. This listing concerns only the discs produced by that label.

The prefix of the catalog number carries with it certain clues about the form of the release. In general, the following rules apply:

ML — Monaural long-playing record

M2L — Set of 2 Monaural long-playing records

D3L — Set of 3 Monaural long-playing records sold for the price of 2

MS — Stereophonic long-playing record

M2S — Set of 2 stereophonic long-playing records

M3S — Set of 3 stereophonic long-playing records

D3S — Set of 3 stereophonic long-playing records sold for the price of 2

M4S — Set of 4 stereophonic long-playing records

MG — Set of 2 stereophonic long-playing records sold at a "bargain" price

MGP — Set of 2 stereophonic long-playing records sold at a "bargain" price

BS — Stereophonic long-playing record issued as a "bonus"

MQ (followed by 5 digits) — quadraphonic long-playing record

MT — Audio cassette
M2T — Set of 2 audio cassettes
M3T — Set of 3 audio cassettes
M4T — Set of 4 audio cassettes
MGT — Audio cassette corresponding to an "MG" record set

MA — 8-track cartridge
MQ (followed by 3 digits) — Reel-to-reel 1/4-track tape

M — Stereophonic long-playing record (newer releases)
M2 — Set of 2 stereophonic long-playing records (newer releases)
M3 — Set of 3 stereophonic long-playing records (newer releases)
M4 — Set of 4 stereophonic long-playing records (newer releases)

S — Stereophonic long-playing record containing a "sound track"
ST — Audio cassette containing a "sound track"
SA — 8-track cartridge of a "sound track"

Y — Stereophonic long-playing record on the "Odyssey" (budget) label
MY — Stereophonic long-playing record on the "Odyssey" label
MYK — Compact disc on the "Odyssey" label
MYT — Audio cassette on the "Odyssey" label

MP — Stereophonic long-playing record on the "Masterworks Portrait" label
M3P — Set of 3 stereophonic long-playing records on the "Masterworks Portrait" label

MPT — Audio cassette on the "Masterworks Portrait" label

IM — Stereophonic long-playing record made from a digital tape

IMT — Audio cassette made from a digital tape

MK — Compact disc
MLK — Compact disc made from a monaural tape
M2K — Set of 2 compact discs
M3K — Set of 3 compact discs
M4K — Set of 4 compact discs

??DC — Compact disc released by "CBS/Sony" in Japan

MXT
M3X   Any catalog number containing an X indicates an
M4X   item sold at a special price. This can be higher
           or lower than normal.

32 11 0045   This pair of numbers (representing mon-
32 11 0046   aural and stereophonic releases, re-
                  spectively) indicates a record on the
                  short-lived "CBS" label. This label was
                  intended to contain material of in-
                  ternational appeal.

In the listings of both composers and producers, credit extends downward until a new name is indicated.

Producer credits carry with them an extra set of problems. In the early days of LP releases, no names were shown on the album. Then, after credit for the producer became standard, an occasional album would emerge without this listing. Sometimes a set that embodied the work of more than one producer would have one or two names missing. This would tend to imply that one producer was taking credit for another's work.

An attempt has been made to straighten out this confusion. If a particular producer has made a contribution to an album but his name was not credited on the jacket, he will be listed within parentheses. A name shown within quotation marks indicates that this credit is printed on the album despite the fact that there is something not completely legitimate about the listing.

Beginning with entry number 113, the compact discs issued by CBS/SONY are listed in a group. These recordings set themselves apart from the main body of foreign releases because of the aggressive position that CBS/SONY assumed very early in the compact disc era. I believe that no other affiliate of CBS Masterworks was responsible for instigating such a large number of original repertoire groupings. Even though it appears that there is occasional exact correspondence with domestic Masterworks releases, the Sony CDs may or may not represent the same "mix" of the original analog tapes.

The listing begins on page 178.

ENTRY NO.	CATALOG NO.	COMPOSER	COMPOSITION	PARTICIPATING ARTISTS	PRODUCER	YEAR OF RELEASE
1	ML 5060 MY 38479 MYT 38479 MLK 38479 MYK 38479	Bach	*Goldberg Variations*		(Howard Scott)	1956
2	ML 5130	Beethoven	Piano Sonatas No. 30 in E Major, op. 109 No. 31 in A♭ Major, op. 110 No. 32 in C Minor, op. 111		(Howard Scott)	1956
3	ML 5186	Bach	Partita no. 5 in G Major Partita no. 6 in E Minor WTC Book 2, Fugue in F♯ Minor WTC Book 2, Fugue in E Major		(Howard Scott)	1957
4	ML 5211	Bach Beethoven	Concerto no. 1 in D Minor Concerto no. 2 in B♭ Major	Leonard Bernstein, Columbia Symphony	(Howard Scott)	1957
5	ML 5274	Haydn Mozart	Sonata no. 3 in E♭ Major Sonata no. 10, K. 330 Fantasia and Fugue, K. 394		(Howard Scott)	1958
6	ML 5298 MS 6017	Bach Beethoven	Concerto no. 5 in F Minor Concerto no. 1 in C Major	Vladimir Golschmann, Columbia Symphony	(Howard Scott)	1958

7	ML 5336	Berg Schönberg Krenek	Sonata Three Pieces, op. 11 Sonata no. 3		(Howard Scott)	1959
8	ML 5418 MS 6096	Beethoven	Concerto no. 3 in C Minor	Leonard Bernstein, Columbia Symphony	(Howard Scott)	1960
9	ML 5472 MS 6141	Bach	Partita no. 1 in B♭ Major Partita no. 2 in C Minor Italian Concerto		(Howard Scott)	1960
10	ML 5578 MS 6178	G. Gould	String Quartet, op. 1	Symphonia Quartet	(Howard Scott)	1960

11	ML 5637
	MS 6237
		Brahms	Intermezzo in E♭ Major, op. 117,
			  no. 1
			Intermezzo in B♭ Minor, op. 117,
			  no. 2
			Intermezzo in C♯ Minor, op. 117,
			  no. 3
			Intermezzo in E♭ Minor, op. 118,
			  no. 6
					(Howard Scott)	1961

			Intermezzo in E Major, op. 116, no. 4 Intermezzo in A Minor, op. 76, no. 7 Intermezzo in A Major, op. 76, no. 6 Intermezzo in B Minor, op. 119, no. 1 Intermezzo in A Minor, op. 118, no. 1 Intermezzo in A Major, op. 118, no. 2		(Joseph Scianni) (Howard Scott)	

ENTRY NO.	CATALOG NO.	COMPOSER	COMPOSITION	PARTICIPATING ARTISTS	PRODUCER	YEAR OF RELEASE
12	ML 5662 MS 6262	Beethoven	Concerto no. 4 in G Major	Leonard Bernstein, New York Philharmonic	(Howard Scott)	1961
13	ML 5738 MS 6338 MP 38785	Bach	*Art of the Fugue* Fugues 1–9		Joseph Scianni	1962 1983
14	ML 5739 MS 6339	Mozart Schönberg	Concerto no. 24 in C Minor Concerto, op. 42	Walter Susskind Robert Craft, CBC Symphony	Howard Scott Joseph Scianni	1962
15	ML 5741 MS 6341 MP 39754 MPT 39754	R. Strauss	*Enoch Arden*	Claude Rains	Joseph Scianni	1962 1985
16	ML 5808 MS 6408	Bach	*The Well-tempered Clavier* Book 1, Preludes and Fugues 1–8		Joseph Scianni (nos. 2, 6) Paul Myers (nos. 1, 3, 4, 5, 7, 8)	1963
17	ML 5898 MS 6498	Bach	Partita no. 3 in A Minor Partita no. 4 in D Major Toccata no. 7 in E Minor		Paul Myers	1963

#	Catalog	Composer	Work	Producer	Year
18	M2L 293 M2S 693	Bach	Partita no. 1 in B♭ Minor Partita no. 2 in C Minor Partita no. 3 in A Minor Partita no. 4 in D Major Partita no. 5 in G Major Partita no. 6 in E Minor	Howard Scott Paul Myers Howard Scott	1963
19	ML 5938 MS 6538	Bach	*The Well-tempered Clavier* Book 1, Preludes and Fugues 9–16	Paul Myers	1964
20	ML 6022 MS 6622 MP 38768 MPT 38768	Bach	Two- and Three-Part Inventions and Sinfonias	Paul Myers Howard Scott	1964 1983
21	ML 6086 MS 6686	Beethoven	Piano Sonatas No. 5 in C Minor, op. 10, no. 1 No. 6 in F Major, op. 10, no. 2 No. 7 in D Major, op. 10, no. 3	Thomas Frost	1965
22	ML 6176 MS 6776	Bach	*The Well-tempered Clavier* Book 1, Preludes and Fugues 17–24	Paul Myers	1965
23	D3L 333 D3S 733	Bach	*The Well-tempered Clavier* Book 1—Complete	"Paul Myers" (Joseph Scianni)	1965
24	M2L 336 M2S 736	Schönberg	Drei Klavierstücke, op. 11 Fünf Klavierstücke, op. 23 Sechs kleine Klavierstücke, op. 19 Suite für Klavier, op. 25	(Howard Scott) Andrew Kazdin Thomas Frost (John McClure), Thomas Frost	1966

ENTRY NO.	CATALOG NO.	COMPOSER	COMPOSITION	PARTICIPATING ARTISTS	PRODUCER	YEAR OF RELEASE
			Klavierstücke, op. 33a & op. 33b		Andrew Kazdin / Thomas Frost	
			Zwei Gesänge, op. 1	Donald Gramm		
			Vier Lieder, op. 2	Ellen Faull	Andrew Kazdin	1966
			Das Buch der Hängenden Gärten, op. 15	Helen Vanni		1984
25	ML 6288 / MS 6888 / MP 38888 / MPT 38888	Beethoven	Piano Concerto no. 5, *Emperor*	Leopold Stokowski, American Symphony	Andrew Kazdin	1966
26	D3L 354 / D3S 754	Bach	Partita no. 1 in B♭ Minor / Partita no. 2 in C Minor		"Paul Myers" (Howard Scott)	1966
			Partita no. 3 in A Minor / Partita no. 4 in D Major / Partita no. 5 in G Major / Partita no. 6 in E Minor		Paul Myers	
			Two- and Three-Part Inventions		(Howard Scott) / Paul Myers	
27	ML 6345 / MS 6945	Beethoven	Piano Sonatas / No. 8 in C Minor, op. 13 / No. 9 in E Major, op. 14, no. 1 / No. 10 in G Major, op. 14, no. 2		Andrew Kazdin	1967

28	ML 6401 MS 7001	Bach	Keyboard Concertos (vol. 1) No. 3 in D Major No. 5 in F Minor No. 7 in G Minor	Vladimir Golschmann, Columbia Symphony	Andrew Kazdin (Howard Scott) Andrew Kazdin	1967
29	ML 6439 MS 7039	Schönberg	Piano Concerto, op. 42	Robert Craft, CBC Symphony	"John McClure" (Joseph Scianni)	1967
30	M2L 367 M2S 767	Schönberg	Various, plus: *Ode to Napoleon Buonaparte* Fantasy for Violin and Piano	Various, plus: Juilliard Quartet, John Horton Israel Baker	(Richard Killough) (Paul Myers)	1967
31	32 11 0045 32 11 0046		*"Canadian Music in the 20th Century"*	Andrew Kazdin		1968
		Morawetz Anhalt Hétu	Fantasy in D Minor Fantasia Variations			
32	ML 6488 MS 7088 MQ 974 DM 359 DMS 359 DT 360	Beethoven	Piano Sonatas (Record Club Release) No. 8 in C Minor, op. 13, *Pathetique* No. 14 in C# Minor, op. 27, no. 2, *Moonlight* No. 23 in F Minor, op. 57, *Appassionata*	Andrew Kazdin		1968

ENTRY NO.	CATALOG NO.	COMPOSER	COMPOSITION	PARTICIPATING ARTISTS	PRODUCER	YEAR OF RELEASE
33	MS 7095	Beethoven (arr. Liszt)	Symphony no. 5		Andrew Kazdin	1968
34	BS 15		"Glenn Gould: Concert Dropout"	John McClure	Andrew Kazdin	1968
35	MS 7096 M 31820 MT 31820 MA 31820	Bach	Goldberg Variations (re-channeled for stereo)		Howard Scott	1968 1973
36	MS 7097	Mozart	Piano Sonatas, vol. 1 Sonata no. 1, K. 279 Sonata no. 2, K. 280 Sonata no. 3, K. 281 Sonata no. 4, K. 282 Sonata no. 5, K. 283		Andrew Kazdin	1968
37	MS 7098	Schönberg	Drei Klavierstücke, op. 11 Fünf Klavierstücke, op. 23 Sechs kleine Klavierstücke, op. 19 Suite für Klavier, op. 25		(Howard Scott) Andrew Kazdin Thomas Frost (John McClure), Thomas Frost	1968
			Klavierstücke, op. 33a and op. 33b		Andrew Kazdin	
38	MS 7099	Bach	The Well-tempered Clavier Book 2, Preludes and Fugues 1–8		Andrew Kazdin	1968

39	MS 7507 MQ 32057 M 39436 MT 39436 MLK 39436	Mozart	*"Mozart's Greatest Hits"* Various, plus: Sonata no. 15, K. 545—First Movement	"Thomas Frost" (Andrew Kazdin)	1969 1973
40	MS 7173	Prokofiev Scriabin	Piano Sonata no. 7 Piano Sonata no. 3	Andrew Kazdin	1969
41	MS 7274	Mozart	Piano Sonatas, vol. 2 Sonata no. 6, K. 284 Sonata no. 7, K. 309 Sonata no. 9, K. 311	Andrew Kazdin	1969
42	MS 7294	Bach	Keyboard Concertos, vol. 2 No. 2 in E Major No. 4 in A Major	Vladimir Golschmann, Columbia Symphony Andrew Kazdin	1969
43	D3S 806 (MS 7325)	Schumann	Various, plus: Quartet in E♭ Major for Piano and Strings	Juilliard Quartet Richard Killough	1969
44	MGP 13	Various, plus Mozart	*"Our Best to You"* Sonata no. 15, K. 545—First Movement	(Various) plus (Andrew Kazdin)	1969

ENTRY NO.	CATALOG NO.	COMPOSER	COMPOSITION	PARTICIPATING ARTISTS	PRODUCER	YEAR OF RELEASE
45	MS 7514 M 39442 MT 39442 MLK 39442	Bach	"Bach's Greatest Hits," vol. 2 Various, plus: WTC Book 1, Prelude and Fugue in C Major WTC Book 1, Prelude and Fugue in C Minor		Various plus Paul Myers	1970
46	MS 7406	Beethoven	"Happy Birthday Ludwig" Various, plus: Sonata no. 8 in C Minor, op. 13, Pathetique (First Movement)		(Various) plus (Andrew Kazdin)	1970
47	MS 7409	Bach	The Well-tempered Clavier Book 2, Preludes and Fugues 9–16		Andrew Kazdin	1970
48	MS 7413 MT 7413 MT 31131 MA 31131	Beethoven	Piano Sonatas (retail release) No. 8 in C Minor, op. 13, Pathétique No. 14 in C♯ Minor, op. 27, no. 2, Moonlight No. 23 in F Minor, op. 57, Appassionata		Andrew Kazdin	1970
49	M 30080	Beethoven	32 Variations in C Minor Variations in F on an Original Theme, op. 34 Eroica Variations, op. 35		Andrew Kazdin	1971

50	Y 30491	Beethoven	Piano Concerto no. 1	Vladimir Golschmann, Columbia Symphony	1971
			Sonata no. 9, op. 14, no. 1	Howard Scott	
				Andrew Kazdin	
51	M 30537	Bach	*The Well-tempered Clavier* Book 2, Preludes and Fugues 17–24	Andrew Kazdin	1971
52	M 30825 MP 39552 MPT 39552	Byrde Gibbons Byrde Gibbons Byrde	First Pavan and Galliard Fantasy in C Allemande, or Italian Ground Hughe Ashton's Ground Sixth Pavan and Galliard "Lord of Salisbury" Pavan and Galliard A Voluntary Sellinger's Round	Andrew Kazdin	1971
53	M 31073	Mozart	Piano Sonatas, vol. 3 Sonata no. 8, K. 310 Sonata no. 10, K. 330 Sonata no. 12, K. 332 Sonata no. 13, K. 333	Andrew Kazdin	1972
54	MG 31261 MGT 31261	Bach	*"The Greatest Hits Album—Bach"* Various, plus: WTC Book 1, Prelude and Fugue in C Major WTC Book 1, Prelude and Fugue in C Minor	Various, plus Paul Myers	1972

ENTRY NO.	CATALOG NO.	COMPOSER	COMPOSITION	PARTICIPATING ARTISTS	PRODUCER	YEAR OF RELEASE
55	MG 31267 MGT 31267	Mozart	*"The Greatest Hits Album—Mozart"* Various, plus: Sonata no. 15, K. 545—First Movement		Various, plus Andrew Kazdin	1972
56	M 31311	Schönberg	Zwei Gesänge, op. 1 Vier Lieder, op. 2 *Das Buch der Hängenden Gärten*, op. 15	Donald Gramm Ellen Faull Helen Vanni	Thomas Frost Andrew Kazdin	1972
57	M 31312	Schönberg	Six Songs for Voice and Piano, op. 3 Two Ballads for Voice and Piano, op. 12 Three Songs for Voice and Piano, op. 48 Two Songs for Voice and Piano, op. 14 Two Songs for Voice and Piano, op. posth. Eight Songs for Voice and Piano, op. 6	Donald Gramm Helen Vanni, Cornelis Opthof Helen Vanni	Thomas Frost Andrew Kazdin	1972
58	S 31333 ST 31333 SA 31333	Bach	*"Music from 'Slaughterhouse Five' "* Concerto no. 5 in F Minor Concerto no. 3 in D Major *Goldberg Variations*, nos. 18 and 25	Vladimir Golschmann, Columbia Symphony	Howard Scott Andrew Kazdin Howard Scott	1972

No.	Catalog	Composer	Work	Performer	Producer	Year
			Brandenburg Concerto no. 4	Alexander Schneider, Rudolph Serkin, Pablo Casals, Marlboro Festival Orchestra	Thomas Frost	
59	M 31512 MP 39128 MPT 39128	Handel	"Komm, heiliger Geist, Herre Gott" Suite no. 1 in A Major Suite no. 2 in F Major Suite no. 3 in D Minor Suite no. 4 in B Minor	Lionel Rogg	Andrew Kazdin	1972
60	D3M 31525	Bach	*The Well-tempered Clavier* Book 2—complete		Andrew Kazdin	1972
61	M 32040 MP 38784 MPT 38784	Grieg Bizet	Piano Sonata, op. 7 Premier Nocturne *Variations Chromatiques*		Andrew Kazdin	1973 1983
62	M 32347 MT 32347	Bach	French Suite no. 1 in D Minor French Suite no. 2 in C Minor French Suite no. 3 in B Minor French Suite no. 4 in E♭ Major		Andrew Kazdin	1973

ENTRY NO.	CATALOG NO.	COMPOSER	COMPOSITION	PARTICIPATING ARTISTS	PRODUCER	YEAR OF RELEASE
63	M 32348	Mozart	Piano Sonatas, vol. 4 Sonata no. 11, K. 331 Sonata no. 15, K. 545 Fantasia in D Minor, K. 397 Sonata in F Major with Rondo, K. 533/494		Andrew Kazdin	1973
64	M 32349 MP 39547 MPT 39547	Beethoven	Piano Sonatas: No. 16 in G Major, op. 31, no. 1 No. 17 in D Minor, op. 31, no. 2 No. 18 in E♭ Major, op. 31, no. 3		Andrew Kazdin	1973 1983
65	M 32350	Hindemith	Piano Sonata no. 1 Piano Sonata no. 2 Piano Sonata no. 3		Andrew Kazdin	1973
66	M 32351 MT 32351 MA 32351	Wagner (arr. Gould)	Die Meistersinger Prelude "Dawn and Siegfried's Rhine Journey" Siegfried Idyll		Andrew Kazdin	1973
67	M 32853 MT 32853	Bach	French Suite no. 5 in G Major French Suite no. 6 in E Major Overture in the French Style		Andrew Kazdin	1974
68	M 32934	Bach	Sonatas for Viola da Gamba and Keyboard Sonata no. 1 in G Major Sonata no. 2 in D Major	Leonard Rose	Andrew Kazdin	1974

No.	Catalog	Composer	Works	Performer	Producer	Year
			Sonata no. 3 in G Minor			
69	M 33265	Beethoven	Bagatelles, op. 33 Bagatelles, op. 126		Andrew Kazdin	1975
70	M 33515	Mozart	Piano Sonatas, vol. 5 Fantasia and Sonata no. 14, K. 475/457 Sonata no. 16, K. 570 Sonata no. 17, K. 576		Andrew Kazdin	1975
71	M2 33971	Hindemith	Sonata for Horn and Piano Sonata for Bass Tuba and Piano Sonata for Trumpet in B♭ and Piano Sonata for Alto Horn in E♭ and Piano Sonata for Trombone and Piano	Philadelphia Brass Ensemble	Andrew Kazdin	1976
72	M2 34226	Bach	Sonatas for Violin and Harpsichord Sonata no. 1 in B Minor Sonata no. 2 in A Major Sonata no. 3 in E Major Sonata no. 4 in C Minor Sonata no. 5 in F Minor Sonata no. 6 in G Major	Jaime Laredo	Andrew Kazdin	1976
73	M 34555	Sibelius	Sonatine, op. 67, no. 1 Sonatine, op. 67, no. 2 Sonatine, op. 67, no. 3 Kyllikki, op. 41		Andrew Kazdin	1977

ENTRY NO.	CATALOG NO.	COMPOSER	COMPOSITION	PARTICIPATING ARTISTS	PRODUCER	YEAR OF RELEASE
74	M2 34578	Bach	English Suite no. 1 in A Major English Suite no. 2 in A Minor English Suite no. 3 in G Minor English Suite no. 4 in F Major English Suite no. 5 in E Minor English Suite no. 6 in D Minor		Andrew Kazdin	1977

75	Y4 34640	Beethoven	Piano Concerto no. 1
			Piano Concerto no. 2
			Piano Concerto no. 3
			Piano Concerto no. 4
				Vladimir Golschmann
				Leonard Bernstein
				  Columbia Symphony
				Leonard Bernstein,
				  New York
				  Philharmonic
					Howard Scott	1977

			Piano Concerto no. 5	Leopold Stokowski, American Symphony	Andrew Kazdin	
76	M2 34597	Hindemith	*Das Marienleben* (original version)	Roxolana Roslak	Andrew Kazdin	1978

77	D5S 35899	Mozart	Piano Sonatas—Complete
			  Sonata no. 1, K. 279
			  Sonata no. 2, K. 280
			  Sonata no. 3, K. 281
			  Sonata no. 4, K. 282
			  Sonata no. 5, K. 283
			  Sonata no. 6, K. 284
					Andrew Kazdin	1979

78   M 35144   Bach
      MT 35144

Sonata no. 7, K. 309
Sonata no. 8, K. 310
Sonata no. 9, K. 311
Sonata no. 10, K. 330
Sonata no. 11, K. 331
Sonata no. 12, K. 332
Sonata no. 13, K. 333
Fantasia and Sonata no. 14,
    K. 475/457
Sonata no. 15, K. 545
Sonata no. 16, K. 570
Sonata no. 17, K. 576
Fantasia in D Minor, K. 397
Sonata in F Major with Rondo,
    K. 533/494   Andrew Kazdin   1979

79   M 35831   Bach
      MT 35831

Toccatas, vol. 1
Toccata in D Major
Toccata in F# Minor
Toccata in D Minor   Andrew Kazdin   1980

Toccatas, vol. 2
Toccata in C Minor
Toccata in G Minor
Toccata in G Major
Toccata in E Minor   Paul Myers

ENTRY NO.	CATALOG NO.	COMPOSER	COMPOSITION	PARTICIPATING ARTISTS	PRODUCER	YEAR OF RELEASE
80	M 35891 MT 35891	Bach	*"Preludes, Fughettas and Fugues"*		Andrew Kazdin	1980
			SIX LITTLE PRELUDES			
			Prelude in C Major			
			Prelude in C Minor			
			Prelude in D Minor			
			Prelude in D Major			
			Prelude in E Major			
			Prelude in E Minor			
			Prelude and Fughetta in D Minor			
			Prelude in G Major			
			Prelude in G Major			
			Fughetta in G Major			
			From NINE LITTLE PRELUDES		Glenn Gould	
			Prelude in C Major			
			Prelude in F Major			
			Prelude in D Minor			
			Prelude in D Major			
			Prelude in F Major			
			Prelude in G Minor			
			THREE LITTLE FUGUES		Andrew Kazdin	
			Fugue in D Major		Glenn Gould	
			Fughetta in C Minor			
			Fugue in C Major			

			Prelude and Fugue in A Minor		
			Prelude and Fugue in E Minor	Andrew Kazdin, "Glenn Gould"	1980
81	M2 35911	Beethoven	Sonata no. 1 in F Minor, op. 2, no. 1 Sonata no. 2 in A Major, op. 2, no. 2 Sonata no. 3 in C Major, op. 2, no. 3 Sonata no. 15 in D Major, op. 28	Andrew Kazdin	1980
82	M2X 35914	D. Scarlatti	*"Silver Jubilee Album"* Sonata in D Major, L. 463 Sonata in D Minor, L. 413 Sonata in G Major, L. 486		
		C. P. E. Bach	Würtemberg Sonata no. 1 in A Minor		
		G. Gould	"So You Want to Write a Fugue"	Vladimir Golschmann Juilliard Quartet Elizabeth Benson-Guy Anita Darian Charles Bressler Donald Gramm	Paul Myers
		Scriabin	2 Pieces, op. 57 (Desir—Caresse dansée)		Andrew Kazdin
		R. Strauss	*Ophelia Lieder*, op. 67 1–3	Elisabeth Schwarzkopf	Paul Myers
		Beethoven (arr. Liszt)	Symphony no. 6—First Movement		Andrew Kazdin
			"A Glenn Gould Fantasy" (interview)		Glenn Gould

ENTRY NO.	CATALOG NO.	COMPOSER	COMPOSITION	PARTICIPATING ARTISTS	PRODUCER	YEAR OF RELEASE
83	M 36672 MT 36672	Bach	*"The Little Bach Book"*			1980
			Goldberg Variations—Aria		Howard Scott	
			Little Preludes nos. 1 and 2		Andrew Kazdin	
			Four Two-Part Inventions (nos. 1, 8, 4, 14)		Paul Myers	
			Partita no. 1—Minuets I, II, and Gigue		Howard Scott	
			English Suite no. 3—Gavottes I and II		Andrew Kazdin	
			WTC Book 1—Preludes and Fugues in B♭ Major and D Major		Paul Myers	
			French Suite no. 5—Gavotte, Bourée, and Gigue		Andrew Kazdin	
			WTC Book 1—Prelude and Fugue in C Major		Paul Myers	
			Fughetta in C Minor		Glenn Gould	
			Prelude in C Major		Andrew Kazdin	
			Five Two-Part Inventions (nos. 10, 3, 13, 6, 15)		Paul Myers	
			French Suite no. 3—Minuet and Trio		Andrew Kazdin	
			French Suite no. 6—Minuet, Bourée, and Gigue			
			English Suite no. 2—Bourées I and II, Gigue			

No.	Catalog	Composer	Work	Performers	Producer	Year
84	IM 37779 IMT 37779 MK 37779	Bach	Goldberg Variations (1982)		Glenn Gould and Samuel H. Carter	1982
85	I2M 36947 M2K 36947	Haydn	"The Six Last Sonatas" Sonata no. 56 in D Major Sonata no. 58 in C Major Sonata no. 59 in E♭ Major Sonata no. 60 in C Major Sonata no. 61 in D Major Sonata no. 62 in E♭ Major		Glenn Gould and Samuel H. Carter	1982 1989
86	IM 37800 IMT 37800 MK 37800	Brahms	Ballade in D Minor, op. 10, no. 1 Ballade in D Major, op. 10, no. 2 Ballade in B Major, op. 10, no. 3 Ballade in B Minor, op. 10, no. 4 Rhapsody in B Minor, op. 79, no. 1 Rhapsody in G Minor, op. 79, no. 2		Glenn Gould and Samuel H. Carter	1983
87	M 37831 MT 37831	Beethoven	Sonata no. 12 in A♭ Major, op. 26 Sonata no. 13 in E♭ Major, op. 27, no. 1		Andrew Kazdin Glenn Gould	1983
88	MY 38524 MYT 38524 MYK 38524	Bach	Concerto no. 1 in D Minor	Leonard Bernstein, New York Philharmonic	Howard Scott	1983
			Concerto no. 4 in A Major Concerto no. 5 in F Minor	Vladimir Golschmann, Columbia Symphony	Andrew Kazdin Howard Scott	1989

ENTRY NO.	CATALOG NO.	COMPOSER	COMPOSITION	PARTICIPATING ARTISTS	PRODUCER	YEAR OF RELEASE
89	MP 38749 MPT 38749	Bach	Italian Concerto English Suite no. 3—Gavottes I and II French Suite no. 5—Gavotte, Bourée, and Gigue English Suite no. 2—Bourées I and II, Gigue Little Preludes nos. 1 and 2 WTC Book 1—Prelude and Fugue in C Major WTC Book 1—Prelude and Fugue in C Minor French Suite no. 3—Menuett and Trio French Suite no. 6—Minuet, Bourée, and Gigue Partita no. 1—Minuets I, II, and Gigue Goldberg Variations—Aria	Howard Scott Andrew Kazdin Paul Myers Andrew Kazdin Howard Scott	1983
90	MP 38752 MPT 38752	Mozart	Concerto in C Minor, K. 491 (Gould) Concerto in C Major, K. 467 (Lhevinne)	Walter Susskind, CBC Symphony Jean Morel, Juilliard Orchestra	Howard Scott Thomas Frost	1983
91	M3X 38610 MXT 38610		"Bach, Volume I"			1984
		Bach	Goldberg Variations (1955)		Howard Scott	

No.	Catalog	Composer	Work	Performers	Producer	Year
92	M4X 38614 MXT 38614	Bach	*Goldberg Variations* (1982) 1982 Interview with Tim Page *"The Glenn Gould Legacy, Volume 1"*		Samuel H. Carter	1984
			Goldberg Variations (1955) Concerto no. 1 in D Minor	Vladislav Slovak, Academic Symphony Orchestra of Leningrad	Howard Scott (unknown)	
			WTC Book 2, Fugue in F♯ Minor WTC Book 2, Fugue in E Major Partita no. 6 in E Minor English Suite no. 2 in A Minor French Suite no. 6 in E Major Toccata in D Major Inventions nos. 6, 13, 4 "Glenn Gould, Concert Drop-Out"	John McClure	Andrew Kazdin Howard Scott Andrew Kazdin Paul Myers Andrew Kazdin	
93	M 38659 MK 38659 IMT 38659	R. Strauss	Sonata, op. 5 5 Piano Pieces, op. 3		Samuel H. Carter Andrew Kazdin and Glenn Gould	1984
94	M2 39099 M2T 39099		*"Bach, Volume 2"*		Andrew Kazdin	1984

ENTRY NO.	CATALOG NO.	COMPOSER	COMPOSITION	PARTICIPATING ARTISTS	PRODUCER	YEAR OF RELEASE
		Bach	French Suite no. 1 in D Minor			
			French Suite no. 2 in C Minor			
			French Suite no. 3 in B Minor			
			French Suite no. 4 in E♭ Major			
			French Suite no. 5 in G Major			
			French Suite no. 6 in E Major			
			Overture in the French Style			
95	MP 39126	Schumann	Quintet for Piano and Strings, op. 44	The Juilliard Quartet	Richard Killough	1984
	MPT 39126		Quartet for Piano and Strings, op. 47			
96	M₃P 39647	Beethoven	Piano Sonatas:		Andrew Kazdin	1984
			No. 1 in F Minor, op. 2, no. 1			
			No. 2 in A Major, op. 2, no. 2			
			No. 3 in C Major, op. 2, no. 3			
			No. 5 in C Minor, op. 10, no. 1			
			No. 6 in F Major, op. 10, no. 2		Thomas Frost	
			No. 7 in D Major, op. 10, no. 3			
			No. 8 in C Minor, op. 13			
			No. 9 in E Major, op. 14, no. 1		Andrew Kazdin	
			No. 10 in G Major, op. 14, no. 2			
			"The Glenn Gould Legacy, Volume 2"			
97	M₃ 39036	Beethoven	Concerto no. 1 in C Major	Vladimir Golschmann, Columbia Symphony	Howard Scott	1985
	M₃T 39036					
	M₃K 39036					

98	M2 39682 M2T 39682	Haydn Beethoven	Sonata no. 59 in B♭ Major Concerto no. 2 in B♭ Major	Vladislav Slovak, Academic Symphony Orchestra of Leningrad	(unknown)
		Mozart	Sonata no. 10, K. 330 Fantasia and Fugue, K. 394		Howard Scott	1985
		Beethoven	Sonata no. 32 in C Minor, op. 111 Sonata no. 30 in E Major, op. 109 Sonata no. 31 in A♭ Major, op. 110		
			"Bach, Volume 3"		
		Bach	English Suite no. 1 in A Major English Suite no. 2 in A Minor English Suite no. 3 in G Minor English Suite no. 4 in F Major English Suite no. 5 in E Minor English Suite no. 6 in D Minor		Andrew Kazdin
99	M2 42104 M2T 42104		*"Bach, Volume 4"*			1986
		Bach	Concerto no. 1 in D Minor	Vladislav Slovak, Academic Symphony Orchestra of Leningrad	(unknown)

ENTRY NO.	CATALOG NO.	COMPOSER	COMPOSITION	PARTICIPATING ARTISTS	PRODUCER	YEAR OF RELEASE
			Concerto no. 2 in E Major	Vladimir Golschmann,	Andrew Kazdin	
			Concerto no. 3 in D Major	Columbia Symphony		
			Concerto no. 4 in A Major			
			Concerto no. 5 in F Minor			
			Concerto no. 7 in G Minor			
100	M3 42107		*"The Glenn Gould Legacy, Volume 3"*		Howard Scott	1986
	M3K 42107				Andrew Kazdin	
	M3T 42107	Brahms	Intermezzi			
			Op. 76, nos. 6–7, op. 116, no. 4		Joseph Scianni	
			Op. 117, nos. 1–3, op. 118, nos. 1, 2, and 6		Joseph Scianni, Howard Scott	
			Op. 119, no. 1		Joseph Scianni	
			Rhapsody, op. 79, no. 1		Samuel H. Carter, Glenn Gould	
		Grieg	Sonata for Piano, op. 7		Andrew Kazdin	
		Wagner (arr. Gould)	*Die Meistersinger* Prelude			
			"Dawn and Siegfried's Rhine Journey"			
		Sibelius	Sonatinas op. 67, nos. 1–3			
		R. Strauss	Sonata, op. 5		Samuel H. Carter	

				1986
101	M3 42150		*"The Glenn Gould Legacy, Volume 4"*	
	M3K 42150			Howard Scott
	M3T 42150	Krenek	Sonata no. 3	Andrew Kazdin
		Schönberg	3 Piano Pieces, op. 11	(John McClure),
			5 Piano Pieces, op. 23	Thomas Frost
			Suite for Piano, op. 25	Howard Scott
				Andrew Kazdin
		Berg	Sonata for Piano, op. 1	
		Hindemith	Sonata no. 3	
		Scriabin	Sonata no. 3, op. 23	
			Sonata no. 5, op. 53	
			2 Pieces, op. 57 (Desir— Caresse dansée)	
				1986
102	M2 42161		*"Bach, Volume 5"*	
	M2T 42161	Bach	Toccata in F♯ Minor	Andrew Kazdin
			Toccata in C Minor	
			Toccata in D Major	
			Toccata in D Minor	
			Toccata in E Minor	Paul Myers
			Toccata in G Minor	Andrew Kazdin
			Toccata in G Major	
				1986
103	M3K 42266	Bach	*The Well-tempered Clavier*	Paul Myers,
	M4 42042		(Books 1 and 2—Complete)	Andrew Kazdin
	M4T 42042			

ENTRY NO.	CATALOG NO.	COMPOSER	COMPOSITION	PARTICIPATING ARTISTS	PRODUCER	YEAR OF RELEASE
104	MK 42267	Bach	*"French Suites—Complete"*		Andrew Kazdin	1986
			French Suite no. 1 in D Minor			
			French Suite no. 2 in C Minor			
			French Suite no. 3 in B Minor			
			French Suite no. 4 in E♭ Major			
			French Suite no. 5 in G Major			
			French Suite no. 6 in E Major			
105	M2K 42268	Bach	*"English Suites—Complete"*		Andrew Kazdin	1986
			English Suite no. 1 in A Major			
			English Suite no. 2 in A Minor			
			English Suite no. 3 in G Minor			
			English Suite no. 4 in F Major			
			English Suite no. 5 in E Minor			
			English Suite no. 6 in D Minor			
			Overture in the French Style			
106	M2 42164 M2T 42164	Bach	*"Bach, Volume 6"*			1987
			Partita no. 1 in B♭ Minor		Howard Scott	
			Partita no. 2 in C Minor			
			Partita no. 3 in A Minor		Paul Myers	
			Partita no. 4 in D Major			
			Partita no. 5 in G Major		Howard Scott	
			Partita no. 6 in E Minor			

No.	Catalog	Composer	Work	Performer(s) / Producer(s)	Year
107	M2K 42269	Bach	*"Toccatas—Complete"* Toccata in F♯ Minor Toccata in C Minor Toccata in D Major Toccata in D Minor Toccata in E Minor Toccata in G Minor Toccata in G Major Two- and Three-Part Inventions	Andrew Kazdin Paul Myers Andrew Kazdin Paul Myers	1987
108	M2K 42270	Bach	*"Keyboard Concertos"* No. 1 in D Minor No. 2 in E Major No. 3 in D Major No. 4 in A Major No. 5 in F Minor No. 7 in G Minor Italian Concerto Art of the Fugue (Fugues 1–9)	Vladislav Slovak, Academic Symphony Orchestra of Leningrad (unknown) Vladimir Golschmann, Columbia Symphony — Andrew Kazdin Howard Scott Andrew Kazdin Howard Scott Joseph Scianni	1987
109	M2K 42402	Bach	Partita no. 1 in B♭ Minor Partita no. 2 in C Minor Partita no. 3 in A Minor Partita no. 4 in D Major	Howard Scott Paul Myers	1987

ENTRY NO.	CATALOG NO.	COMPOSER	COMPOSITION	PARTICIPATING ARTISTS	PRODUCER	YEAR OF RELEASE
			Partita no. 5 in G Major		Howard Scott	
			Partita no. 6 in E Minor			
			SIX LITTLE PRELUDES		Andrew Kazdin	
			Prelude in C Major			
			Prelude in C Minor			
			Prelude in D Minor			
			Prelude in D Major			
			Prelude in E Major			
			Prelude in E Minor			
			Prelude and Fughetta in D Minor			
			Prelude in G Major			
			Prelude in G Major			
			Fughetta in G Major			
			From NINE LITTLE PRELUDES		Glenn Gould	
			Prelude in C Major			
			Prelude in F Major			
			Prelude in D Minor			
			Prelude in D Major			
			Prelude in F Major			
			Prelude in G Minor			
			THREE LITTLE FUGUES		Andrew Kazdin	
			Fugue in D Major		Glenn Gould	

110	M2K 42414	Bach	Fugue in C Minor Fugue in C Major		
			Prelude and Fugue in A Minor Prelude and Fugue in E Minor		
			Sonatas for Viola da Gamba and Keyboard	Leonard Rose	Andrew Kazdin 1987

			Sonata no. 1 in G Major
			  Sonata no. 2 in D Major
			  Sonata no. 3 in G Minor		

			Sonatas for Violin and Harpsichord	Jaime Laredo	

			Sonata no. 1 in B Minor
			  Sonata no. 2 in A Major
			  Sonata no. 3 in E Major
			  Sonata no. 4 in C Minor
			  Sonata no. 5 in F Minor
			  Sonata no. 6 in G Major		

111	MBK 42527	Bach	Partita no. 4 in D Major Italian Concerto Toccata in E Minor		Paul Myers Howard Scott Paul Myers, "Andrew Kazdin" 1988
112	MYK 38524	Bach	Concerto no. 1 in D Minor Concerto no. 4 in A Major Concerto no. 5 in F Minor	Leonard Bernstein Vladimir Golschmann Columbia Symphony	Howard Scott Andrew Kazdin Howard Scott 1989

ENTRY NO.	CATALOG NO.	COMPOSER	COMPOSITION	PARTICIPATING ARTISTS	PRODUCER	YEAR OF RELEASE
113	38DC 54	Brahms	Ballade in D Minor, op. 10, no. 1 Ballade in D Major, op. 10, no. 2 Ballade in B Major, op. 10, no. 3 Ballade in B Minor, op. 10, no. 4 Rhapsody in B Minor, op. 79, no. 1 Rhapsody in G Minor, op. 79, no. 2		Glenn Gould and Samuel H. Carter	1983
114	35DC 105	Beethoven	Sonata no. 12 in A♭ Major, op. 26 Sonata no. 13 in E♭ Major, op. 27, no. 1		Andrew Kazdin Glenn Gould	1983
115	00DC 120 00DC 121 00DC 122 00DC 123	Bach	The Well-tempered Clavier (Books 1 and 2—Complete)		Paul Myers, Andrew Kazdin	1984
116	56DC 148 56DC 149	Bach	"English Suites—Complete" English Suite no. 1 in A Major English Suite no. 2 in A Minor English Suite no. 3 in G Minor English Suite no. 4 in F Major English Suite no. 5 in E Minor English Suite no. 6 in D Minor		Andrew Kazdin	1984
117	56DC 153 56DC 154	Bach	"French Suites—Complete" French Suite no. 1 in D Minor French Suite no. 2 in C Minor		Andrew Kazdin	1984

No.	Catalog	Composer	Title	Producer	Year
			French Suite no. 3 in B Minor	Samuel H. Carter	1984
			French Suite no. 4 in E♭ Major	Andrew Kazdin and Glenn Gould	
			French Suite no. 5 in G Major		
			French Suite no. 6 in E Major		
			Overture in the French Style		
118	38DC 172	R. Strauss	Sonata, op. 5		
			Five Piano Pieces, op. 3		
119	56DC 178	Bach	Partita no. 1 in B♭ Minor	Howard Scott	1984
	56DC 179		Partita no. 2 in C Minor	Paul Myers	
			Partita no. 3 in A Minor	Howard Scott	
			Partita no. 4 in D Major		
			Partita no. 5 in G Major		
			Partita no. 6 in E Minor		
120	56DC 186	Bach	Toccata in F♯ Minor	Andrew Kazdin	1984
	56DC 187		Toccata in C Minor		
			Toccata in D Major		
			Toccata in D Minor		
			Toccata in E Minor	Paul Myers	
			Toccata in G Minor	Andrew Kazdin	
			Toccata in G Major		
121	56DC 265	Bach	SIX LITTLE PRELUDES	Andrew Kazdin	1984
	56DC 266		Prelude in C Major		
			Prelude in C Minor		

ENTRY NO.	CATALOG NO.	COMPOSER	COMPOSITION	PARTICIPATING ARTISTS	PRODUCER	YEAR OF RELEASE
			Prelude in D Minor			
			Prelude in D Major			
			Prelude in E Major			
			Prelude in E Minor			
			Prelude and Fughetta in D Minor			
			Prelude in G Major			
			Prelude in G Major			
			Fughetta in G Major			
			From NINE LITTLE PRELUDES		Glenn Gould	
			Prelude in C Major			
			Prelude in F Major			
			Prelude in D Minor			
			Prelude in D Major			
			Prelude in F Major			
			Prelude in G Minor		Andrew Kazdin	
			THREE LITTLE FUGUES		Glenn Gould	
			Fugue in D Major			
			Fughetta in C Minor			
			Fugue in C Major			
			Prelude and Fugue in A Minor			
			Prelude and Fugue in E Minor			
			Two- and Three-Part Inventions		Paul Myers	

122	56DC 267 56DC 268	Haydn	"The Six Last Sonatas" Sonata no. 56 in D Major Sonata no. 58 in C Major Sonata no. 59 in E♭ Major Sonata no. 60 in C Major Sonata no. 61 in D Major Sonata no. 62 in E♭ Major	Glenn Gould and Samuel H. Carter	1984
123	00DC 269 00DC 270 00DC 271 00DC 272	Mozart	"Piano Sonatas—Complete" Sonata no. 1, K. 279 Sonata no. 2, K. 280 Sonata no. 3, K. 281 Sonata no. 4, K. 282 Sonata no. 5, K. 283 Sonata no. 6, K. 284 Sonata no. 7, K. 309 Sonata no. 8, K. 310 Sonata no. 9, K. 311 Sonata no. 10, K. 330 Sonata no. 11, K. 331 Sonata no. 12, K. 332 Sonata no. 13, K. 333 Fantasia and Sonata no. 14, K. 475/457 Sonata no. 15, K. 545 Sonata no. 16, K. 570	Andrew Kazdin	1984

ENTRY NO.	CATALOG NO.	COMPOSER	COMPOSITION	PARTICIPATING ARTISTS	PRODUCER	YEAR OF RELEASE
			Sonata no. 17, K. 576			
			Fantasia in D Minor, K. 397			
			Sonata in F Major with Rondo, K. 533/494			
124	00DC 273	Beethoven	Piano Sonatas			1985
	00DC 274		No. 1 in F Minor, op. 2, no. 1		Andrew Kazdin	
	00DC 275		No. 2 in A Major, op. 2, no. 2			
	00DC 276		No. 3 in C Major, op. 2, no. 3			
	00DC 277		No. 5 in C Minor, op. 10, no. 1		(Thomas Frost)	
	00DC 278		No. 6 in F Major, op. 10, no. 2			
			No. 7 in D Major, op. 10, no. 3			
			No. 8 in C Minor, op. 13		Andrew Kazdin	
			No. 9 in E Major, op. 14, no. 1			
			No. 10 in G Major, op. 14, no. 2			
			No. 12 in A♭ Major, op. 26			
			No. 13 in E♭ Major, op. 27, no. 1			
			No. 14 in C# Minor, op. 27, no. 2			
			No. 15 in D Major, op. 28			
			No. 16 in G Major, op 31, no. 1			
			No. 17 in D Minor, op. 31, no. 2			
			No. 18 in E♭ Major, op. 31, no. 3			
			No. 23 in F Minor, op. 57			

No.	Catalog	Composer	Work	Performers	Producers	Year
125	56DC 279 56DC 280	Beethoven (arr. Liszt) Wagner (arr. Gould)	Symphony no. 5 Symphony no. 6—First Movement *Die Meistersinger* Prelude "Dawn and Siegfried's Rhine Journey" *Siegfried Idyll*		Andrew Kazdin	1985
126	75DC 451 75DC 452 75DC 453	Bach	"Keyboard Concertos" No. 1 in D Minor No. 2 in E Major No. 3 in D Major No. 4 in A Major No. 5 in F Minor No. 7 in G Minor	Leonard Bernstein Vladimir Golschmann, Columbia Symphony	Howard Scott Andrew Kazdin	1986
127	75DC 454 75DC 455 75DC 456	Bach	The Six Sonatas for Violin and Harpsichord Sonata no. 1 in B Minor Sonata no. 2 in A Major Sonata no. 3 in E Major Sonata no. 4 in C Minor Sonata no. 5 in F Minor Sonata no. 6 in G Major The Three Sonatas for Cello and Piano Sonata no. 1 in G Major Sonata no. 2 in D Major Sonata no. 3 in G Minor	Jaime Laredo Leonard Rose	Howard Scott Andrew Kazdin	1985

ENTRY NO.	CATALOG NO.	COMPOSER	COMPOSITION	PARTICIPATING ARTISTS	PRODUCER	YEAR OF RELEASE
128	75DC 457 75DC 458 75DC 459	Beethoven	*"Complete Piano Concertos"* Piano Concerto no. 1 Piano Concerto no. 2 Piano Concerto no. 3 Piano Concerto no. 4 Piano Concerto no. 5	Vladimir Golschmann Leonard Bernstein, Columbia Symphony Leonard Bernstein, New York Philharmonic Leopold Stokowski, American Symphony	Howard Scott Andrew Kazdin	1986
129	75DC 460 75DC 461 75DC 462	Beethoven Brahms	32 Variations in C Minor Variations in F on an Original Theme, op. 34 *Eroica* Variations, op. 35 Bagatelles, op. 33 Bagatelles, op. 126 Intermezzo in E$\flat$ Major, op. 117, no. 1 Intermezzo in B$\flat$ Minor, op. 117, no. 2 Intermezzo in C$\sharp$ Minor, op. 117, no. 3		Andrew Kazdin Howard Scott	1986

No.	Catalog	Composer	Work	Performer	Year
			Intermezzo in E♭ Minor, op. 118, no. 6	Joseph Scianni	
			Intermezzo in E Major, op. 116, no. 4		
			Intermezzo in A Minor, op. 76, no. 7		
			Intermezzo in A Major, op. 76, no. 6		
			Intermezzo in B Minor, op. 119, no. 1		
			Intermezzo in A Minor, op. 118, no. 1		
			Intermezzo in A Major, op. 118, no. 2	Howard Scott, Richard Killough	
		Schumann	Quartet in E♭ Major for Piano and Strings	Juilliard Quartet	1986
130	75DC 465	Hindemith	Piano Sonata no. 1	Andrew Kazdin	1986
	75DC 466		Piano Sonata no. 2		
	75DC 467		Piano Sonata no. 3		
			Sonata for Horn and Piano	Philadelphia Brass Ensemble	1976
			Sonata for Bass Tuba and Piano		
			Sonata for Trumpet in B♭ and Piano		
			Sonata for Alto Horn in E♭ and Piano		
			Sonata for Trombone and Piano		
131	ooDC 468	Schönberg	Drei Klavierstücke, op. 11	Howard Scott	1986
	ooDC 469		Fünf Klavierstücke, op. 23	Andrew Kazdin	
	ooDC 470		Sechs kleine Klavierstücke, op. 19	Thomas Frost	
	ooDC 471		Suite für Klavier, op. 25	John McClure, Thomas Frost, Andrew Kazdin, Joseph Scianni	
			Klavierstücke, ops. 33a and 33b		
			Piano Concerto, op. 42	Robert Craft, CBC Symphony	

ENTRY NO.	CATALOG NO.	COMPOSER	COMPOSITION	PARTICIPATING ARTISTS	PRODUCER	YEAR OF RELEASE
			Fantasy for Violin and Piano	Israel Baker	Paul Myers	
			Ode to Napoleon Buonaparte	Juilliard Quartet, John Horton	Richard Killough	
			Zwei Gesänge, op. 1		Thomas Frost	
			Vier Lieder, op. 2	Donald Gramm Ellen Faull		
			Das Buch der Hängenden Gärten, op. 15	Helen Vanni	Andrew Kazdin	
			Six Songs for Voice and Piano, op. 3	Donald Gramm	Thomas Frost	
			Two Ballads for Voice and Piano, op. 12	Helen Vanni, Cornelis Opthof	Andrew Kazdin	
			Three Songs for Voice and Piano, op. 48	Helen Vanni		
			Two Songs for Voice and Piano, op. 14			
			Two Songs for Voice and Piano, op. posth.			
			Eight Songs for Voice and Piano, op. 6			
132	75DC 472	Handel	Suite no. 1 in A Major		Andrew Kazdin	1986
	75DC 473		Suite no. 2 in F Major			
	75DC 474		Suite no. 3 in D Minor			
			Suite no. 4 in B Minor			
		Byrde	First Pavan and Galliard			
		Gibbons	Fantasy in C			
			Allemande, or Italian Ground			
		Byrde	Hughe Ashton's Ground			
			Sixth Pavan and Galliard			

No.	Composer	Work	Performers	Producer	Year
	Gibbons	"Lord of Salisbury," Pavan and Galliard		Howard Scott	
	Byrde	A Voluntary / Sellinger's Round		Andrew Kazdin	
	Mozart	Concerto no. 24 in C Minor	Walter Susskind, CBC Symphony		
	D. Scarlatti	Sonata in D Major, L. 463 / Sonata in D Minor, L. 413 / Sonata in G Major, L. 486			
	C. P. E. Bach	Würtemberg Sonata no. 1 in A Minor			
	G. Gould	"So You Want to Write a Fugue"	Vladimir Golschmann / Juilliard Quartet / Elizabeth Benson-Guy / Anita Darian / Charles Bressler / Donald Gramm	Paul Myers	
	Scriabin	2 Pieces, op. 57 (Desir—Caresse dansée)		Andrew Kazdin	
	R. Strauss	Ophelia Lieder, op. 67, 1–3	Elisabeth Schwarzkopf	Paul Myers	
133 30DC 717	Bach	Goldberg Variations (1982)		Glenn Gould and Samuel H. Carter	1986
134 30DC 738	Mozart	Piano Sonatas / Sonata no. 2, K. 280 / Sonata no. 8, K. 310 / Sonata no. 9, K. 311		Andrew Kazdin	1986

ENTRY NO.	CATALOG NO.	COMPOSER	COMPOSITION	PARTICIPATING ARTISTS	PRODUCER	YEAR OF RELEASE
			Sonata no. 11, K. 331 Fantasia in D Minor, K. 397			
135	50DC 757	Bach	The Well-tempered Clavier (Book 1)		Paul Myers	1986
136	30DC 780	Bach	Two- and Three-Part Inventions and Sinfonias		Paul Myers	1986
137	30DC 800	Bach	Partita no. 4 in D Major Italian Concerto Toccata in E Minor		Paul Myers Howard Scott Paul Myers	1986
138	75DC 816 75DC 817 75DC 818	Hindemith R. Strauss	Das Marienleben (original version) Enoch Arden	Roxolana Roslak Claude Rains	Andrew Kazdin Joseph Scianni	1986
139	60DC 822 60DC 823	Grieg Sibelius Bizet Scriabin Prokofiev	Piano Sonata, op. 7 Sonatine, op. 67, no. 1 Sonatine, op. 67, no. 2 Sonatine, op. 67, no. 3 Kyllikki, op. 41 Premier Nocturne Variations Chromatiques Piano Sonata no. 3 Piano Sonata no. 7		Andrew Kazdin	1986
140	66DC 5147 66DC 5148 66DC 5149	Bach	The Well-tempered Clavier (Books 1 and 2—Complete)		Paul Myers, Andrew Kazdin	1988